A Meadow Murder

A Jan Christopher
Mystery

Helen Hollick

TAW RIVER
PRESS

A Meadow Murder
A Jan Christopher Mystery - Episode 4
By Helen Hollick

ISBN: 978-1-7392720-6-7 A Meadow Murder (paperback)
978-1-7392720-7-4 A Meadow Murder (ebook)

Published by Taw River Press 2023
https://www.tawriverpress.co.uk

READERS' COMMENTS

"If you enjoy cozy mysteries, then this is definitely for you." *Historical Novel Society Review*

"I sank into this gentle cosy mystery story with the same enthusiasm and relish as I approach a hot bubble bath, (in fact this would be a great book to relax in the bath with!) and really enjoyed getting to know the central character, a shy young librarian, and the young police officer who becomes her romantic interest. The nostalgic setting of the 1970s was balm, so clearly evoked, and although there is a murder at the heart of the story, it was an enjoyable comfort read." *Debbie Young, author of the Sophie Sayers cosy mysteries*

"A delightful read about a murder in North-East London. Told from the viewpoint of a young library assistant, the author draws on her own experience to weave an intriguing tale." *Richard Ashen – South Chingford Community Library*

Amazon Readers:

"An enjoyable read with a twist in who done it. I spent the entire read trying to decide what was a clue and what wasn't... Kept me thinking. I call that a success."

"A delicious distraction... What a lovely way to spend an afternoon!"

"I really identified with Jan – the love of stories from an early age, and the careers advice – the same reaction I got – no one thought being a writer was something a working class girl did! The character descriptions are wonderfully done."

"Brilliant! I'm so enjoying Helen's well-researched murder mystery. I'm not giving anything away here, except to say there's lots of nostalgia, and detail that readers of a certain age (me included) will lap up. A jolly good read. In my opinion, it would make a great television series."

To my friend, Heather,
for her good company beneath the 'gaze-bo'
or with toes stretched towards the log fire...
(and for sharing tea, cake and the occasional glass of bubbly)

1

UP THE LANE

The drive down from London to North Devon for ten days of blissful summer holiday had been long and tiring, but without incident. Unless you count me nearly bursting my boiler, desperate to spend a penny. Laurie Walker, my policeman fiancé, managed to find me a suitable bush just in time. We'd arrived at his parents' lovely old farmhouse at about 2 p.m. and were made heartily welcome by his mum Elsie, and dad Alf, with cups of tea and enormous wedges of chocolate cake. We sat out in the garden, under the shade of a wooden gazebo, which Elsie laughingly called her 'gaze-bo' or, more officially, The Go Outside in mock pretence of a tiny, private English pub, on account of Alf using it to enjoy a pint or two of his special home-brewed beer. (It was actually good stuff, but rather strong.) An old oak tree stood not far behind the structure and we sprawled in the wicker garden chairs, breathing in the fresh Devonshire air and listening to the surrounding country sounds: birds singing, bees buzzing, a breeze whispering through the oak leaves, and Bess, the Labrador, sniffing around for dropped crumbs.

No traffic, no aeroplanes, no shouting. No criminals for Laurie to investigate, and no public demanding this, that or the other from me. I'm Jan, (short for January as that's the month I was born, but I try to avoid using it). I'm a library assistant in a public library, and while I enjoy my job – and the unlimited access to books – the General Public can be somewhat wearing at times. Especially when their books are overdue and they don't see why they have to pay a fine because of it. The commonest indignant protest is usually, 'I pay my rates. That means I pay your wages!' Yes, well, my colleagues and I pay council rates, too. Except, technically, I don't as I live with my uncle, DCI Toby Christopher and Aunt Madge. They pay rates and I give them a percentage of my monthly wage for housekeeping. I think that counts, don't you?

The fresh air had woken me up; I'd dozed in the stuffy car, but I could see that Laurie was tired, he was almost nodding off in the warm sunshine. He roused when his mum offered another cup of tea. We'd left London at some silly-o'clock time when the sun had only just got out of bed – although as a Detective Sergeant in the police force, he was used to long, odd, hours so he refused a third cup, stood up, stretched, and suggested a gentle walk up the lane. I was fine with the 'gentle' but the 'up' bit was somewhat daunting as here in Devon 'up' is *very* 'up'. Mrs Walker said she was getting low on tea, and if we didn't mind going to the village shop, which, of course we didn't, could we get a couple of packets of P.G. Tips for her?

It was a beautiful afternoon. After changing into suitable shoes, Laurie and I set off arm-in-arm up the hill. Even though she wanted to come, we didn't take Bess with us, because of the heat and she was starting to get old. Dogs are always enthusiastic about prospective 'walkies' but are not savvy enough to work out the consequence of a hot day combined with more than a mile to the village. Not a great distance, but for an elderly dog on a hot day it would be too much for her, despite it being nicely shaded beneath the trees bordering the lane – hazel, ash, oak, beech, birch, holly. Their leafy branches formed ideal curved archways for us to stroll under.

There were two magnificent elm trees halfway up the lane. Laurie stopped to inspect them for any sign of the Dutch elm disease that was sweeping through much of southern Britain. The epidemic killing these beautiful old trees was a fungus spread by an invasive beetle. Such a shame. Nothing could be done to protect or save the trees.

"They look healthy enough," Laurie said, taking my hand and walking on. He looked back over his shoulder. "Though, I wonder how long before they succumb to this wretched disease."

The hedges to either side were smothered in ferns and wildflowers: foxgloves, dog roses, honeysuckle, campion, stitchwort, valerian – they're the ones I know. There were a lot more, including the inevitable nettles and brambles – although at least the latter would produce plump, ripe blackberries come early autumn.

We stopped at the wooden gate into the bottom end of Top Meadow.

"Ssh!" Laurie said, putting his fingers to his lips. "Go quietly to the gate and look over."

He held back a long bramble so that I could step across the grass to the garden-type gate, and pointed. In the shadow of an oak tree, two rabbits were nibbling at the clover and grass. I had to smile, remembering my favourite *Little Grey Rabbit* stories from childhood. One of those books was an earliest memory: I distinctly recall coming out from Walthamstow Junior Library, clutching a *Little Grey Rabbit* book, thrilled because it was one I had not read. I was four. I liked to think that, in the same way, children today left 'my' library at South Chingford clutching a much-loved treasure to read, enjoy and remember. My only slight disappointment was that these bunnies looked more brown than grey.

Laurie touched my arm and pointed again, whispered, "Look, over there in the field, where the land starts to slope down towards the woods."

At first, I couldn't see anything, but then a movement caught my attention and I saw them – two Fallow deer does browsing in the long grass, their distinctive spotty hides providing superb camouflage. I must have made some sort of appreciative sound because the bunnies scattered, their white scuts flashing as they disappeared into the concealing tall grass and meadow flowers that would soon be cut for hay. Alerted, the deer also turned tail and fled down the slope to vanish into the safe shadows of the woods at the bottom of the hill.

"I love it here," I said to Laurie as I slipped my arm through his and we ambled on up the lane to stop again at the top to lean on a larger, wooden farm gate to admire the panoramic view. No sign of the deer now, for the 'V' dip of woodland in this gentle part of the valley was hidden by the sloping terrain; only the top halves of the trees could be seen from up here. Laurie explained that a stream ran down through the woods, all the way from the village up on the ridge to the wide river meandering through the valley – the River Taw, which gave the area its name.

"You can see some of the river from your bedroom window," he said, "and part of the Tarka Line railway as it sweeps round a long bend."

I nodded. I'd watched several trains chugging by the last time I'd been here, at Christmas. It had been quite exciting at night to see the train's line of carriage lights curving around the track, and hearing the rhythmic *clickety-clack* as it trundled over the wooden bridge crossing the river. It was like looking down on my own personal section of a model railway.

"What are the buildings I can see from my window? The ones near the track? It all looks too spread-out to be a farm?" I asked – intentionally prolonging the conversation in order to get my breath, and to put off the next part of our walk.

"That would be Four Horseshoes, a racehorse training yard run by Jack Woollen. I expect we'll see some of his horses tomorrow, when we go to Newton Abbot races."

I was looking forward to that, and the pleasure of my Aunt Madge and Uncle Toby coming down to Devon for a long weekend break, starting with us all enjoying an afternoon at the racecourse.

Here, from the gate, we could see the entire half-circle of 'our' bit of the Taw Valley: on the far side, the verdant, rounded hills sloped upward in an almost mirror image of our side of the 'V', except, over there a few more farms and houses were dotted about, their white cob walls gleaming in the afternoon sunshine. Devon is primarily an agricultural county, with a large proportion of wildlife found on the farmland and the moors – Exmoor, Dartmoor and Bodmin Moor. The valleys and rolling hills make the county less suitable for the intensive agriculture which made huge changes to the English landscape in the 1940s and '50s. Here, sheep and cattle grazed in the grassy, green fields patchworked, here and there, by yellow meadows of sunbaked grass that looked ready to be cut and baled as hay.

"Ralph Greenslade, from Lower Valley View Farm, will cut soon," Laurie said, as if he had read my thoughts. "Possibly tomorrow, then it'll be all hands on deck in a couple of days to help bring the bales in, especially if the weather starts to look unsettled."

I looked up at the almost cloudless blue sky. "Is it likely to change?" I asked, sceptically.

"It can change overnight down here in the West Country," Laurie said. "It's not likely just yet, but in a couple of days we could be threatened with thunderstorms – although this valley, for some reason, seems to escape the worst of it. The air currents, I suppose. They tend to go round the side of us. Barnstaple and South Molton get the downpours with the accompaniment of thunder and lightning more than we do."

I was relieved to hear it; I wasn't too keen on thunderstorms.

Two buzzards were circling, high, high up, plaintively mewing to each other.

"You can tell the weather by the buzzards," Laurie said, also watching them.

"Oh? How?"

He grinned. "If you see a buzzard, it isn't raining."

"Oh, very funny." I aimed a reprimanding light kick at his ankle.

"No, seriously; they don't like the rain. But aren't they magnificent? I like to think they're calling to each other for no other reason than to express their joy at being up there, gliding above this wonderful landscape."

"Or they could be saying, 'Look at those two humans leaning on the gate down there. How sad that they can't fly'."

Laurie grinned and took my hand in his then we set off for the next part of the lane which dipped down a short way, then trudged upward again before joining

6

Mallard Lane, a steady gradient of about half a mile to the ridge and the village of Chappletawton.

"But why do we need to help with the hay?" I asked, knowing how heavy bales of hay were, wondering why hay making would involve us, and, if it did, how much trudging up and down hill would be required. None of which would be my idea of a relaxing holiday.

"We're not obliged to help at all," Laurie explained, "but we have a laugh working together, and Top Meadow actually belongs to Dad. But we like to join in when we can. Those fields running alongside the lane we've just walked up are ours too, but Dad lets Ralph use them. One day – one distant day I might add – when Valley View Farm becomes mine and I've retired from the police, I'll keep sheep and cattle and make the hay for myself." He grinned, and knowing I was a 'horse' person, added, "and keep a pony or two."

I was slightly puzzled as I knew Mr Greenslade's name was spelt r.a.l.p.h, which I had always pronounced to rhyme with 'Alf', but Laurie had said 'Rafe'. I plucked up courage to ask why, fearing I'd show my ignorance.

Laurie's helpful explanation emphasised the quirks of the English language. "Americans use Ralf, as in 'Alf', but we dopey Brits use the ph spelling and say 'Rafe', to rhyme with 'safe'. No idea why."

A sort of penny dropped. "Oh, that's why Aunt Madge always says *Rafe* for Vaughan Williams, the composer!"

My cheeks reddened a little as I felt an embarrassed chump. I'd somehow always assumed the two different pronunciations referred to two different names.

We walked on. I hit on what I thought would be a sensible question to ask. "How many acres does Valley View have?"

"Fifteen in all."

"Oh." I was astonished by that. When I'd previously stayed for Christmas, I had assumed the property was the house, orchard, a small woodland copse and the garden; it had never occurred to me that some of the nearby land belonged to the Walkers as well.

"Where is the baled hay kept?" I asked tentatively, uneasily thinking of the steep hills again.

"From our field? It's stored in the big barn opposite the house, the one next to our garage."

"And do we have to walk up and down with bales of hay?" OK, that sounded as lame a question as it actually was.

Laurie laughed. "No, silly, it's stacked onto a large trailer. Play your cards right, you'll get to ride the trailer down the hill. It's great fun. Very clattery and swayey coming back up with the trailer empty; you cling onto the bars for dear life. Great fun."

I reserved judgement on that.

Talk of the devil, as the saying goes, in Mallard Lane we met a tractor trundling towards us, driven by Ralph – *Rafe* – Greenslade himself.

"Af'noon young Laurie, Miss Christopher. Fine day!"

I noted that, as with most Devonshire people who spoke with the local accent, Mr Greenslade pronounced an 'f' as a 'v' sound. So *vine* day. Laurie often slipped into the dialect as well, despite living in a London suburb for quite a while now.

"It certainly is, Mr Greenslade. I was just telling Jan about cutting the hay in our meadow."

"Oh, arr, be cuttin' 'er s'af'noon I reckon. Get 'er all in afore the rain blows up."

"We'll be there to help," Laurie answered. "When do you think it'll be?"

"Mond'y, I 'spec. Give 'er time to dry nice. Got 't be proper dry, else it could combust a'cause o' the heat damp hay generates."

"Monday it is then," Laurie said, giving a half salute.

We squeezed into a gap in the hedged bank and Laurie admired the rattling and huffing, bright red Massey-Ferguson tractor as it crawled past us.

"I've always liked tractors," he said. "During the summer holidays, from when I was about ten years old, Ralph used to let me drive his old one round the fields. Great way to learn to drive."

"That was good of him," I answered, but added sceptically, "isn't ten a bit young?"

"Yes, he's a good chap. Most farming kids learn to drive the tractors at an early age. It's part of country life. Did you know that Harry Ferguson was an Irish engineer?" he added with an enthusiastic grin. "He developed the modern agricultural tractor, the first four-wheel drive Formula One car and was the first Irishman to build and fly his own aeroplane."

No, I didn't know that, and wasn't sure that I even wanted to know it, but I made a few suitably impressed noises about the information, then asked, hoping that I didn't show too much trepidation, "Is it hard work, helping with the hay?"

"Not as hard as it used to be for people in the past when everything was done by hand. Now it is hard, but good exercise. Think how trim your figure will get!" he teased, then seeing me scowl at the reference to my puppy-fat waistline gave me a reassuring kiss. "But I love you just as you are."

I grinned at him. "When you're in a hole, DS Walker, stop digging."

The last farm we came to before turning towards the village at Mallard's Cross, was Higher Valley View, which was completely boarded up and had a large 'FOR SALE' sign on the sagging front gate. I had last seen the place at New Year, and given the sadnesses that had soaked into it – at least two murders – I wondered if anyone would want to buy it. Laurie told me that a property developer was rumoured to be interested.

"He'll pull the lot down, that which hasn't already collapsed of its own dilapidated accord, and build family houses instead. He'll make a decent profit, I expect."

We reached the main road at Mallard's Cross and turned left towards the village. I say 'main' road, it was just about wide enough for two cars to squeeze past each other slowly and carefully. 'Our' lane was even narrower, a single track which, in places, seemed even narrower because of the robust hedging. Devon lanes are fascinating because of the hedges and views – when you can see over the hedges that is – but the lanes are not known for their ample width or straight lines. The old thing about 'you can tell a Roman Road because of its straightness' doesn't apply to Devon. Obviously, the Romans didn't get much further into this West Country than Exeter. No wonder the smugglers of the past used to bring their strings of ponies carrying contraband kegs of brandy and tobacco along these concealing byways. *Four and twenty ponies, trotting through the dark...* I could well imagine it. And by the time we'd reached the road I did wish I had a pony to ride, rather than walk. My feet and calves were definitely complaining, but thankfully, the road became flat as we approached the village.

Several of the cottages lined along either side of the road were stereotypical, white-walled cob with bow windows and thatched roofs, with roses and honeysuckle arching round the front doors, their front gardens blooming with things like foxgloves and hollyhocks.

Inspired, I started singing a well-known, traditional folk song. *"How many flowers bloom and grow, in an English country ga...ar...den? I'll tell you now, of some that I know, and those I miss I'm sure you'll pa...ar...don.* I can't remember who made a record of it," I said, "I know it was played a lot on the radio, and Aunt Madge often sings it when she's gardening."

"I've no idea either, but I do know the song."

The nearest cottage had a black cat curled up on one of the windowsills. He opened one eye and stared disdainfully at us.

"I don't think he liked my singing," I said.

"Probably doesn't understand your London accent, it's very different from the Devonshire one."

I wasn't sure if that was a polite diversion, or he agreed with the cat.

We turned right onto The Ridgeway, which made me smile as, back in Chingford, I lived along a very different Ridgeway. The name, 'Ridgeway', so I'd been told, indicated an ancient track that followed a ridge atop a line of hills, (surprise, surprise!). The other old name for an ancient thoroughfare is High Street, 'Street' being an Anglo-Saxon term while 'way' is Celtic. I've no idea where 'road' comes from. Being facetious I'd say Roman, as in 'Roman Road', but that's nonsense as the term would be 'Via' in Latin. *Via Appia*, the Appian Way, one of the earliest and most important Roman roads, connecting Rome to southeast Italy.

I only know this because one of my favourite films is *Spartacus*, starring Kirk Douglas and Tony Curtis alongside Olivier and the wonderful Peter Ustinov. (It is here that you stand up and shout, 'I'm Spartacus!') If you're interested, the film is based on fact: in 71 BC, six thousand slaves were crucified along the more than one-hundred-mile length of the *Via Appia* from Rome to Capua as punishment for their attempted rebellion and bid for freedom. When it came to killing people, they were rather a vicious lot, those Romans.

And in case you are wondering, I know these things, not because of my next-to-useless schooling, but because I work in a public library. I read books and discover a ton of random, useless but interesting, information. I must add, I've learnt more since leaving school in 1969 than all the years that I attended the awful place.

On the corner of the road was a red telephone box with a man inside talking animatedly on the phone, his back to us, waving his free arm about like Don Quixote tilting at a windmill. He wasn't shouting but he was plainly angry, saying something like, "I've told you. No, I haven't got it." He then angrily banged his fist on the glass and a girl, aged about twelve and shrieking with laughter, darted out from the bushes growing behind the box.

"Oi! You being a nuisance, Mary-Anne Culpin?" Laurie shouted after her as she ran across the road to the playground field opposite the shop.

"Little terror," Laurie said, hiding a smile as we turned towards the shop-cum-Post Office. "Kids'll be kids, though, I suppose."

2

WORSE THAN THE KIDS

The shop door was propped open to let in a breeze on this hot afternoon. Inside, Heather, the shopkeeper and postmistress, was standing behind the counter looking somewhat frazzled. She flicked back a lock of damp, blonde hair from her forehead and puffed her cheeks as we walked in.

"Oh, it's only you young Laurie, and you Jan dear. I thought it was those pesky children or Dotty Dorothy come back again. Did you not see her? She's only just left. Driven me barking with her silliness."

Laurie laughed. I looked blank.

"Mrs Dorothy Clack," Laurie explained. "Lives in Meadow View, the first cottage as you come into the village. Her husband is a salesman of some sort, rarely at home. She's a sweet lady, but..."

Heather butted in. "But she is as dotty as a polka-dot bikini. It isn't surprising that her other half is rarely here with her. Quiet chap, I've only seen him once or twice since they moved here a few years ago. It's my opinion that he's got someone else on the side, if you know what I mean. Can't say as I blame him, Dorothy must drive him up the wall. Yesterday, she was certain that George Dill's scarecrow was following her around the village. Didn't matter how many times I told her that George moves the thing about in an attempt to keep the crows from his crop. Now, she's adamant that she's seen a leprechaun in Windfall Woods. I quote: 'A little man, sitting on a log.' He apparently took one look at her, jumped up, shouted, 'Begorrah!' and disappeared."

"Well, it is a lovely public footpath through those woods," Laurie said, still laughing, "though she's more likely to meet a poacher, not a leprechaun."

"I don't suppose you came up that way? Saw anything odd?" Heather queried. "Just in case it was a poacher hanging around? I've no objection to anyone taking a rabbit or pheasant for the supper table, or farmers keeping the foxes at bay, but shooting the deer this time of year when the does have fawns at foot? If I ever caught anyone, I'd shoot them myself." She paused, grinned. "The poachers I mean, not the deer."

Laurie advised that that wouldn't be a good idea, and asked for two packets of tea, which Heather fetched. He added, "We walked up the lane, not through the woods, but we can go back that way."

I selected some picture postcards of views of Exmoor and pretty thatched cottages with various straw figures decorating the ridges, such as hares, pheasants, geese and foxes, and followed Heather as she went to the post office counter to get the stamps to go with them. I was fiddling with my shoulder bag to get my purse out when a shadow blotted the light from the open door. I paid my money and Heather, noticing the newcomer, dramatically rolled her eyes. I put the stamps and cards in my bag and turned to see who had come in.

"Hello! It's PC Walker, isn't it? I remember you from a couple of summers back," boomed a tall, very good-looking man in his fifties. He had an upper-class British accent tinged with a slight American slant. "I had heard, young sir, that you had upped sticks a while ago and left us for the exciting lure of the Big Smoke?"

Then the man saw me and raised his straw Trilby hat. He looked slightly familiar but beyond realising that he had been the cross man in the telephone box, I couldn't place him.

"And who is this delightful young lady?" he gushed. "Do I perceive an angel before my eyes? '*O, speak bright angel! For thou art as glorious to this afternoon, being o'er my head as is a wingèd messenger of heaven*'."

I blushed, but found the courage to reply, "Well, strictly speaking it is the night not afternoon, for Romeo is talking about the stars and the moon, but: '*As is a wingèd messenger of heaven to the white wondering eyes of mortals that fall back to gaze on him when he crosses the slow moving clouds and sails upon the heart of the wind*'." My returned quote was almost perfect.

The man beamed and clapped his hands. "By the Bard, you know your Shakespeare my sweet young maid!"

I smiled and curtseyed. (Properly, I might add, without wobbling – my Aunt Madge had been a debutante; she'd expertly taught me the tricky art.) Then explained, "It's Romeo's speech about Juliet as she stands, oblivious to his presence, on her balcony. We did the play at school."

The gentleman stepped forward, took my hand and kissed it in an old-fashioned way. "Ah, and you took the part of the fair Juliet!"

I laughed. "No, I was the prompter for when the other girls forgot their lines. Which most of them did. Frequently." I didn't add that I had been far too shy and scared to actually *act*, or that by the time we got to the third and last night, I'd whispered nearly every line

15

in the entire play as no one had bothered to learn anything properly.

Laurie proffered his hand, which the man took and shook heartily. "I'm a Detective Sergeant now, sir, and yes, I moved to London, but I'm down here on holiday with my fiancée, Jan. Miss Jan Christopher, meet Oliver de Lainé, the actor."

Oh my goodness! I finally realised why he was familiar. Oliver de Lainé was an English-born actor who had starred in many prestigious Hollywood films. He'd even had two Oscar nominations, although I couldn't recall anything he'd been in recently. That explained the American tinge, though.

"Mr de Lainé is here on holiday too," Heather explained, a little tartly, I thought. "He's rented the pub's caravan *every* summer for the entire season these last several years." She didn't sound too approving. I wondered why, but did not think it polite to ask.

"It is a very comfortable caravan, behind a very welcoming pub, with a very obliging landlord and landlady," Mr de Lainé responded. "And I like it because it is secluded and private."

"And not too far to stagger home from the bar," Heather muttered. Adding even quieter under her breath, "And cheap."

"No filming this time of year, then, sir?" Laurie enquired.

"Nay, my dear boy, I rest over the summer. Far too hot in California, and I enjoy the seasonal beauty of this charming valley."

"And the English horse racing," Heather added. She was back behind the main counter. "What more can I do for you Oliver? You were in here not twenty minutes ago."

"That I was, dear lady, that I was." He patted his jacket pockets; he was wearing a light linen suit, nicely tailored. Savile Row, I assumed. "But I seem to have mislaid my little black address book somewhere during the afternoon. I wondered if it had fallen from my pocket whilst I was within your fine premises?"

He looked hopefully at the floor, as we all did. No address book did we spy. From one pocket he produced a gentleman's pigskin wallet and a Yale key. He laid both on the counter and from the other, took out a packet of cigarettes and a brightly coloured matchbook, along with a hank of baling twine which he handed to Heather.

"Throw this in the bin, would you please, dear lady? I do wish farmers would not leave the stuff lying around. It tangles with birds and mammals; does untold damage to the poor things."

He pulled the lining from both pockets. "Empty as a leaking pot. I wondered if I had dropped my little book when I took out my kerchief to give to that wretched tyke of a boy. His dripping nose was disgusting."

"Peter Culpin. The snotty nose is as false as old Bart Goodly's teeth," Heather harrumphed. "It's a regular ploy his older sister makes him use. Let the disgusting green stuff build up whenever someone is in the shop, knowing a handkerchief will be produced by an irritable adult. Blow loudly, make a fuss to create a distraction. Meanwhile, Mary-Anne, his wily minx of a sister, pockets a bar of chocolate."

Laurie frowned. "Want me to have a word with their parents?"

Heather shook her head. "No, I keep an eye on them now. Nothing seems to be missing this time. I think the little madam is realising that I'm getting wise to her game. Dorothy though... Goodness but she drove me round the bend today, going on and on with her silly nonsense about scarecrows and leprechauns. Two weeks ago it was flying saucers over the valley. Turned out to be the 624 Volunteer Gliding Squadron from Chivenor, doing night-time training."

"My address book?" Oliver de Lainé interrupted as he replaced his belongings into his jacket pockets. "Mrs Clack was here, I seem to recall, drinking tea over in your charming café corner. Would she have picked it up and handed it to you, perhaps? It is important, and er, highly private. It contains all my acting contacts. Larry Olivier, Dickie Burton, the beautiful, dear, Liz Taylor. Such eyes! Charlton Heston, Jimmy Stewart… Several directors – Hitch, of course."

As a namedropper, this chap took the biscuit.

"Dorothy was here, yes; her weekly treat to herself, a full cream tea, though I can't get across to her that it isn't the Devon way to put the jam on a scone first. She didn't hand me anything, but I'll ask when I next see her, which I hope will not be too soon. Better still, go and ask her yourself," Heather said decisively, and with a rather disdainful sniff.

"I tried," Mr de Lainé responded. "There appears to be no one at home. I knocked several times."

"It's quite likely that she's bird watching somewhere," Heather advised. "She's always off on some sort of nature project. Her last obsession was bluebells. Digging up the invasive Spanish Bluebells that are threatening our English variety."

I smothered a giggle. In my mind I saw the World War Two Home Guard platoon from TV's *Dad's Army*, pointing their guns at a patch of invasive bluebells, with Corporal Jones and his fixed bayonet saying, "They don't like it up 'em," while Captain Mainwaring ticked off the young Private Pike, with a muttered, "Stupid boy."

"Perhaps you dropped the book in the phone box, Mr de Lainé?" Laurie suggested, giving me a quizzical glance because of the amused snort that I was trying to suppress.

"I looked in there, and along the road. No sign of it," Mr de Lainé said, gloomily. "It's black leather, with a silver clasp. A racehorse embossed on the cover. My sister gave it to me, so it is rather special."

My giggles under control, I returned his hopeful stare with as much sympathy as I could muster.

"Oh well, maybe it will turn up." He didn't sound too hopeful. "However, would you and your fiancé grant me the pleasure of joining me for dinner this evening Miss Christopher? There's nothing I enjoy better than young company."

"That would be nice," I said when Laurie hesitated to answer.

"Maybe later in the week?" my fiancé finally said, without much enthusiasm. "We only got here today, and my parents expect us for dinner tonight. Then we have some outings arranged for the next few days."

"Later in the week it is then." The actor raised his hat, clicked his heels together and gave me a theatrical bow, then headed for the door having to sidestep as a woman was entering, manoeuvring a large pram.

Heather whispered to me. "Take care. Dinner with that one will end in him conveniently having forgotten his wallet, and you paying the bill."

"Them kids be outside making a nuisance of themselves," the woman complained as she wheeled the pram further in. "I told 'em they shouldn't be playing around in Mr Dill's field. They need their legs smacked if you ask me."

"I'll have a word," Laurie suggested. "Perhaps a policeman will have some influence."

"That Mary-Anne Culpin is a bad 'un," the woman complained. "Always up to some mischief or other, she is. Leads her brother and the other village children astray with her jokes an' pranks."

"I'll see what I can do," Laurie repeated. Tea packets in his jacket pockets, my postcards in my shoulder bag, we said goodbye and set off towards Valley View Lane. We'd not gone more than a few yards when we saw a cuddly toy rabbit abandoned in the dusty road. Laurie retrieved it. "I'm sure this wasn't here earlier," he said, looking over his shoulder towards the shop. "I wonder if it belongs to the baby in that pram?" He gave me a quick kiss on the cheek and jogged back towards the shop. "Shan't be a jiffy!" he called.

I looked around for the girl, Mary-Anne, and her brother, but there weren't any children in sight, so I wandered over to a gateway to look at two rather magnificent bay hunters grazing in the field beyond. Then I heard raised voices, not shouting, but two men further along the road were arguing. One was Oliver de Lainé. He was stabbing a finger into the shoulder of a small, skinny man, dressed in an old, green tweed jacket and faded jeans. I couldn't hear much as they were too far away, but I did catch some words when de Lainé's voice rose higher.

"I told you not to come up here, and I also told you, you wormy runt, that I haven't got it! Comprendi? Savvy? Understand?" Gone was the refined actor's English, instead a coarseness that matched the nasty expression on his face.

The small man sneered a retort but all I overheard was, "I want what's mine or I'm..." I didn't hear the last. The man spun on his heel and stamped angrily in my direction. Over his shoulder he hurled a particularly rude expletive, which, fortunately, muffled by a tractor coming round the corner. I recognised an Irish accent, though. He had to step aside for the tractor to pass; in doing so bumped into me.

He growled and snarled, "Watch where y' be goin'!" and stormed off through the gate and onto the footpath that led across Mr Dill's field towards the woods on the far side.

The tractor chuntered on, obscuring the road. When I had a clear view again, de Lainé had gone and Laurie was leaving the shop, *sans* toy bunny, but with two Wall's choc ices instead.

I didn't tell him about the incident; I was too busy licking at an already dripping ice cream, and dribbling melting chocolate down my chin.

3

MEETING WORZEL

Laurie opened the gate and led the way onto the footpath. I was slightly hesitant as this was the direction that foul little man had gone, but I figured he was probably well ahead by now, and anyway, he would be no match for Laurie, so I forgot about him.

"The footpath goes through the woods and further on, sort-of runs parallel with Valley View Lane, but on the far side of the fields. We'll come out opposite our house," Laurie explained as he shut the gate and took my hand in his, then added with a chuckle, "and it's downhill nearly all the way."

I was relieved to hear it.

Halfway across the field we met a raggedy scarecrow wearing a torn jacket and shabby trousers stuffed with straw to give him some shape, and a battered hat set atop a face painted on a white paper sack. He wasn't doing a very good job at scaring crows, because there were lots of them cawing at us from up in the trees. Or maybe they were rooks? I've no idea how to tell the difference, but 'scarerook' doesn't sound quite right, does it?

"Is this the one Dotty Dorothy claimed was following her?" I asked, inspecting the straw man.

"Probably. He looks rather wobbly, doesn't he? George Dill hasn't pushed his support in that well." Laurie stood the scarecrow upright, wedging him firmer into the ground. "Can't have you all skew-whiff can we mate? Makes it look like you've had too much cider."

"Hello Worzel," I said to the scarecrow, giving one of his gloved hands at the end of his jacket sleeves a little shake. "He doesn't look much like the illustrations in the children's books."

"Maybe he smartens himself up of an evening when no one is around because he has a date arranged with Aunt Sally?" Laurie suggested.

"Oh, you've read the books then?"

"Of course. I loved *Worzel Gummidge,* and *Just William,* when I was a kid."

I kissed him (Laurie, not Worzel) for no reason except he had liked the same stories that I'd liked. "And *Swallows and Amazons*?" I suggested, cocking my head to one side enquiringly. "*Better drowned than duffers. If not duffers won't drown.*"

"Ah, I remember that quote! John, Susan, Titty and Roger Walker? How could I not have read about them with a surname like that? As kids, we messed about in boats down on the river, pretending to be Swallows, Amazons or the boys of the Norfolk Broads' Coot Club."

"The Death or Glories."

"Them too."

I mock-swiped at him. "They're the same children, you chump."

Laurie laughed, put his hands round my waist and twirled me around. "I know that. I was teasing you. We were also the Secret Seven, or the Famous Five, depending on mood and weather."

"I wanted to be one of the Woodentops from telly."

"Crikey, that takes me back a bit! Children's TV, *Andy Pandy, Muffin the Mule, Rag, Tag and Bobtail. Tales of the Riverbank.*"

"I don't think the *Tales* were part of the same *Watch with Mother* series? I hated Andy Pandy. He was such a drip."

"*Flob-a-lob,*" Laurie wobbled about pretending to be one of the *Flowerpot Men* with the peculiar way they talked and walked. "*Wee..eed!*" he quoted.

When we stopped laughing, he asked, "Why the *Woodentops?*"

"I loved Spotty Dog the Dalmatian – 'the very biggest, spottiest dog you ever did see'! I learnt to whistle because of the *Woodentops*. The boy *Woodentop* was whistling in one of the episodes and I was so impressed, I sat on the backdoor step for hours trying and trying until I managed to do it."

"You do know," Laurie chuckled as he took my hand and we walked on, "that you are distinctly showing your age? Those shows were on BBC TV ages ago."

"Well, the 1950s and '60s," I corrected with a laugh. "I'm not *that* old you know!"

We ambled towards the far gate and appreciated the cool shade of the trees beyond. I did glance back at the scarecrow; I can't be certain, but did he wink at me?

4

INTO THE WOODS

These woods, Laurie told me, were a long ribbon of trees that meandered for three miles downhill to either side of a wide stream that was not big enough to be called a river, but too deep to be a brook, its source bubbling up from an underground spring just inside the first stand of trees and eventually feeding into the River Taw. The water was low because of the summer dry spell; even so, there were babbling currents, jets and rills where the water hurried over or around pebbles, stones and small rocks. Plants, ferns and such, smothered the banks; trees drooped their branches into the sparkling water that glinted and twinkled beneath the leaf-dappled sunlight. In a small, rocky pool that we came to, I could see little silvery fish darting about.

The air beneath the trees was heavy with the heady scent of summer. Dozens of birds were chattering or squabbling in the tree canopy, and the overgrowth to each side of the footpath was swarming with bees and butterflies. A squirrel saw us coming and darted up a birch tree, then sat on a branch scolding us for startling him.

The footpath itself was wide enough for us to walk

hand-in-hand, and as we passed another pool, I stopped to scoop up a handful of water to drink – sweet, crisp water, but also extremely cold, despite the heat of the afternoon. Laurie grabbed my arm and pointed downstream. "Ssh – look. A kingfisher."

I caught a fleeting glimpse of bright metallic blue – Kingfisher Blue – then it was gone.

"But it was tiny!" I exclaimed. "I thought they were about the size of blackbirds."

"No, they're not much bigger than a robin."

A little further on, the trees thinned out into a grassy clearing. A fallen tree made an ideal seat across one corner and I took full advantage to rest there a moment.

Laurie sat next to me, his arm round my waist, and explained that this spot was kept looking nice as a memorial to the female pilot of a British plane that came down during the war.

"She got into trouble taking it to RAF Chivenor up on the north coast. The engine caught fire and she could easily have baled out, but she was flying over the village and stayed aboard to steer clear as best she could. She came down here, in these woods. The whole plane went up in flames. Her with it."

He pointed to a gravestone marker, which I went over to read.

"She's buried here? 'Avril Woollen 1922-1943. Died whilst saving many lives.' Goodness, she was only twenty-one."

Laurie nodded. "Yes. A girl with local connections. Her uncle was the owner of the race training stables. He died in 1960; his son, Jack, runs it now. There's quite a few cousins of his in the West Country, a big family, the Woollens. I think she came from the Bristol branch."

"I know of the WRAF but didn't know that women flew planes during the war?"

"Women's Royal Air Force? Oh yes, they are well known, but the women who ferried planes were members of the uniformed civilian service, the ATA – the Air Transport Auxiliary, so there were quite a few ladies taking planes from A to B – which freed up the men to do the actual fighting. There also the Land Army, helping to keep farming going, and women took over the canal boats too; kept essential goods transported to and fro. As well as working in the munitions factories and such. My aunt, Dad's eldest sister, Lizzie, was a porter for Great Western Railway. She told us lots of stories, such as how she helped get injured passengers off a bombed train in 1942, and she occasionally worked as a blackout attendant. Her job was to travel on the trains to check that the blinds were always down from dusk to dawn."

"I wonder if your aunt knew George Duffield? You know, the man on my book delivery round whose brother was murdered back in January? He was a train driver for Great Western."

"She might have done. Very probably did, in fact. She was Mrs Elizabeth Grant then, not Walker, married before the war. Her husband copped it during the D-Day landings. I never knew him, of course."

"You said 'us'?" I queried. "Who do you mean?"

"Me and her three children when we had family Christmases together as kids. Aunt Lizzie died a few years back. She was good fun. My cousins are all married now, young families of their own."

"We'll have to invite them to our wedding," I rashly declared.

Laurie squeezed my hand. "That would be nice. You'll like Vi and Betsy. Colin's in Australia. He and his wife went there as Ten Pound Poms in the early sixties.

According to the occasional letter and the annual Christmas card, they're doing well."

There were some flowers in an old earthenware pot beside the grave marker, fairly fresh for they were not quite wilted. On impulse I took the pot and refilled it with clean water, then picked a few more flowers and added them to the arrangement before putting the pot back against the lichen-covered headstone. They wouldn't last long, but I wanted to show my respect for the young woman called Avril.

Laurie had walked off a little way and suddenly started grumbling loudly, bending down to pick things up from the grass.

"Cigarette butts," he complained, showing me the collection in his hand along with a discarded, empty matchbook with a bright red and orange pattern on it. "Apart from the fire risk with everything being as dry as it is, George Dill often tethers his two nanny goats here to keep the grass short and the brambles and nettles at bay. These things could harm the goats if they ate them."

"That's good of Mr Dill," I said, looking round for any more offensive debris.

"Ah, well," Laurie explained, "this is his land, and local gossip has it that he did his courting twenty years ago in this spot." He chuckled. "Or another version is that he killed and buried his annoying brother here."

I gasped and looked suitably shocked. Perhaps Farmer Dill wasn't as good-hearted as I'd thought?

Laurie laughed, shook his head. "It isn't true. His brother lives in blissful contentment in the Scilly Isles."

Laurie wrapped the butts and matchbook in his handkerchief and put them safely in his pocket.

Beyond the clearing, the stream changed direction to run along the other side of a wire boundary fence and skirted an old, fallen oak. Laurie pointed out a badger's sett excavated below the roots of the dead tree.

"It's in use," he said. "You can tell by the smooth sides around the entrance hole, caused by their frequent in and outs and the tell-tale soiled bedding scattered around. Unlike foxes, badgers are clean animals. They like freshly made beds."

"I've never seen a badger," I confessed.

"They're big things, not small cuddly teddy bears, and they can be quite aggressive. People think they eat vegetation and worms, which they do, but they're omnivores, so will eat almost anything, from dead carcases to fruit, bulbs and birds' eggs. Mice, rats, rabbits, frogs, toads, and hedgehogs. One broke into Mum's henhouse a few years back. It ripped the door off and killed the lot."

"How do you know it was a badger, not a fox?" I asked.

"Paw prints in the mud by the hen house."

I suppose I should have guessed that for myself.

The stream fell away from a small waterfall into another shallow pool, and then turned back onto our side of the wire fence, bubbling merrily along, with the steep slopes of fields rising up on each side of this narrow, isolated valley.

"This is our land now," Laurie told me as he helped me scrabble over a stile. Through the crowding trees, I could see the bottom end of Top Meadow, rising away up the hillside to our right towards the distant gate and lane beyond. The tractor sound was nearer and suddenly, over the brow of the hill I saw the red Massey-Ferguson come into view.

"Ah, Ralph's started cutting the hay. We'll walk up the lane again this evening; we might catch a glimpse of a barn owl looking for homeless mice."

We had to stoop under a beech tree bough that had

fallen during the spring storms, then the path headed upward again, proving a bit of a scramble to ascend because of the encroaching undergrowth. We were well above the stream now, looking down on it through the tangled greenery of leaves, bushes and branches. I noticed something really odd on a branch; peering closer, I stepped back horrified. It looked as if some awful person had nailed a handful of human ears along the dead wood.

Laurie chuckled at my revulsion. "It's only Jelly Ear, or *Auricularia auricula-judae* to use its Latin terminology – fungi. I was quite interested in mycology when I was at school."

I wrinkled my nose in disgust. "Is it edible? Though, even if it is, I don't think I'd eat it."

"Tell you the truth, I can't remember if it is or not. It doesn't look tempting does it? Ah, that one over there," he pointed to a white-spotted, red fungus that I recognised. "That's Fly Agaric, traditionally used as an insecticide by breaking the cap up and sprinkling it into saucers of milk."

"And favoured by elves and fairies as picnic tables and stools," I added, "and is poisonous."

"Yes, but it's more known for its hallucinogenic properties. Human deaths from it are extremely rare, though I don't think it's something to experiment with. This one's a bit early; they usually appear late summer or into autumn. I guess the weather this year has suited it. Did you know that it was commonly pictured on Victorian and Edwardian Christmas cards as a good luck symbol? It's thought that the colours were the inspiration behind Santa's red and white suit. Before then, he always wore green."

Laurie's information was interesting, but I decided to stick to eating good, sensible mushrooms.

5

OH DEER!

It was glorious being together, ambling hand-in-hand along the path with nothing to worry about, the cares of the world resting on someone else's shoulders for a while. The *chum, chum, chum,* sound of the tractor up on the hillside behind us, the birds trilling and the bees buzzing. Ewes nearby were calling to their almost-grown lambs. There was a yappy dog barking somewhere over to the left, probably from the cottage in the next lane along, glimpsed through the hedgerows from 'our' lane. In the distance, a cow was lowing. Absolute heaven!

The stream was running merrily along several feet below the path, then suddenly it disappeared, plunging over rocks to cascade down about eight feet into a large pool. I laughed and slithered down a low part of the bank. I couldn't resist the temptation: off came my shoes and socks, I rolled up my jeans as best I could, set down my shoulder bag and, skirting round the edge of the rippling pool, started to climb up the waterfall, to the side of the ribbon of white, frothing water.

"Mind! Those rocks are slippy!" Laurie warned, watching from the bank.

"I've never climbed a waterfall before," I called back. "This is wonderful!"

He laughed. "Well, it's not exactly Niagara Falls, is it?"

Triumphant, I stood at the top, grasping an overhanging branch to steady myself. The white-spumed, gushing waterfall looked a long way down from up here and somehow, I had to descend it again – the banks to either side were too steep to climb up, and anyway, were overgrown with ferns, nettles and brambles. Going down the waterfall itself, backwards and feeling for footholds with my toes, would not be quite as easy as the going up had been – as I soon discovered. I got a little wet, but Laurie gallantly rolled up his trousers and stood, shoe and sock-less, ankle-deep in the pool to steady me down the last few feet. (He claimed that his assistance had nothing whatsoever to do with his hands firmly placed on my hips, either side of my bottom.)

We dried our feet with our socks, then put our shoes back on. The socks were damp, but without them, even though we were not far from home, we would both have quickly got blisters.

We walked on. Laurie stopped to inspect a section of broken fence. "Deer have brought it down, I expect," he said wiggling a loose fence post. I wandered on to what looked to me like a huge mass of rhododendron bushes. I later discovered that's exactly what they were: years and years ago, well before the Great War, there had been a small shepherd's cottage in this part of the woods, and the bushes had been planted in the back garden.

Laurie pointed out another, larger badgers' sett, which looked very much in use.

Rounding the mass of rhododendron bushes, I caught my breath and realising that I was alone, shouted in alarm. "Laurie! Come quick! Laurie, oh the poor thing!"

A deer was caught fast in the wire fence. I started to run, but Laurie seized my arm and, in a lowered voice, urged me to keep still. Initial instinct made me want to shake him off, the trapped animal urgently needed help, but he was right, and sense kicked in.

"We need to go calmly and quietly," Laurie explained, "else we'll frighten her more than she already is." He was fishing in his jacket pocket as he spoke, brought out a Swiss Army Knife, and selected one of the many blades. "This'll do, it can be pliers or a wire cutter."

"Her?" I queried. "Not a 'he'?"

"No, she's a doe, let's hope she doesn't have a fawn nearby, although it doesn't look like she's old enough yet. She doesn't seem to have been tangled here for long, either." He squatted down in order to assess the situation and minimise his size, motioned for me to do the same.

Slowly, Laurie removed his lightweight summer jacket and carefully put the contents of the pockets in a pile. "Here's what we'll do," he said. "I'll approach her quietly, throw my jacket over her head and then pin her down. You take the knife and as quickly as you can, cut through the wire strand caught round her leg. Only be careful, she might kick."

I knew what he meant. I was used to my Aunt Madge's horses, and while they didn't usually kick, I had been on the receiving end of a few bruising blows from iron-shod hooves when something had startled them.

"She'll jump up and run fast the moment we release her, so be ready," Laurie warned.

Bending low, he wriggled forward, jacket in hand and rugby-tackled the deer as he flung his jacket and himself over her. I ran forward and with one hand gripping her leg to keep her still, started on the wire. I was breathing hard from exertion and excitement – and, not fear; apprehension perhaps? The adrenalin rush, sparked by concern? I pressed the small wire cutters harder, biting my lower lip in concentration. It wasn't an easy job.

"Almost done," I panted. "The wire's giving... I think..."

"As soon as you're finished jump back out of the way and I'll let her up."

I nodded. The wire snapped apart. "Done!" I went to move away, and stumbled backwards, landing on my backside just as Laurie let go of her and simultaneously yanked his jacket aside. The deer leapt to her feet, kicked out, then bounded away, seemingly none the worse for wear.

Laurie was rolling on the ground, groaning, his knees bent, hands in a somewhat personal position.

I shouldn't have laughed, probably did so because of the shock. "It's just as well she wasn't a horse with shoes on," I giggled. "That would have hurt even more!"

Laurie grimaced and staggered to his feet, said through gritted teeth, "At the moment, don't even *think* about starting a family one day."

I gathered up Laurie's belongings and slipped everything back into his jacket pockets. Laurie wound the cut wire round the post so that it didn't trail. It was only afterwards, as we walked slowly on (Laurie hobbling and slightly bent over at first), that it occurred to me: the Irishman who had been arguing with de Lainé in the village must have come this way. There were no other paths, unless he'd waded through the stream, brambles and nettles to climb over the wire fencing into the adjoining fields. But if he had stayed on *this* path, he would have seen the trapped deer – and had totally ignored her.

Thank goodness that we'd decided to walk home through the woods and found the poor creature, but I'll not repeat the words that rumbled through my mind about that horrid man. They were not exactly polite or ladylike.

6

A DAY AT THE RACES

The prospect of a day at the races was exciting for two reasons: one was that I had never been to watch live horse racing, and the other was that my aunt and uncle were coming down by train to join us for a long weekend. We – me, Laurie and his mum and dad – were up early, Bess duly fed and walked, and the scullery door left on the latch so that Mrs Greenslade from down the hill could call by and let her out a couple of times during the day for a run. We would never leave doors open back home in Chingford, but everyone did it here in the country. I suppose that was the advantage of living in the middle of nowhere down long, narrow lanes. Not exactly a 'quick getaway' for potential burglars, especially as more often than not it's likely there would be sheep, cattle, or a tractor blocking the exit. Or a car coming the other way which meant one of the drivers would have to reverse to a suitable passing place.

Dressed in 'smart casual', we set off. This was to be a special treat for Laurie's mum, Elsie, as it was her birthday the next day. Naturally, we hoped that she would enjoy herself. The sun was shining, tempered by a gentle, cool breeze, so the weather looked favourable for a good day out.

The train down to Exeter St David's was exciting too. It was a small train with only two carriages and as the station, Umberleigh, was unmanned Laurie had to put his arm out to signal for it to stop. We piled in and found seats, and Laurie pointed out various things to me as we clickety-clacked along, which included the Four Horseshoes racing yard and a glimpse of 'our' house, on the side of the valley, its white walls shining in the morning sun. I know it sounds silly, but it really was quite thrilling to see the house from this angle – from train to house instead of house to passing train.

At Exeter St David's we had a short wait for the London 'down' train on which my aunt and uncle would be aboard. Trains *away* from London, are 'down', while trains *to* London are 'up', which is why most people say 'going up to London,' even if they are travelling north to south. The expected train trundled in almost on time and we easily found Aunt Madge and Uncle Toby in the First Class carriage where our seats had been reserved and paid for by my uncle as a special treat. The usual greeting of hugs and kisses and the asking of, "Did you have a good journey down from London?" before we made ourselves comfortable for the next stage of the journey.

Uncle Toby remarked that the British Rail Full English breakfast hadn't been too bad, if a little greasy, but the railway tea was not to be recommended. Aunt Madge laughed and reminded him that, from experience, she'd told him to ask for coffee, but he hadn't taken heed.

Uncle Toby winked at me. "I seem to recall your aunt saying that the coffee was just as bad."

The views as we travelled along this next leg of the journey were impressive. From the carriage we looked across the estuary towards Exmouth, with the sun sparkling on the blue sea, little boats bobbing on the high tide and the distant beach already looking quite busy, even though it was not yet the school summer holidays. And then we reached Dawlish.

What is a more spectacular word than 'spectacular'? Apart from the view, the track along the sea front, built originally by Isambard Kingdom Brunel, was 'spectacular'. It seemed, in places, that we were almost in the sea itself, except where the track passed through grand archways tunnelled through the red sandstone cliffs.

Dawlish had several literary connections. Jane Austen spent a holiday there and complained about its 'pitiful and wretched library,' which she mentions several times in *Sense and Sensibility*. Being a library assistant, I appreciated the probably justified criticism. Nicholas Nickleby in Dickens' novel inherited a farm near Dawlish, and Keats wrote *Dawlish Fair*, a poem about the seduction of a Devon maid. ('Maid' being a dialect word for girl, not a servant.)

We soon reached Newton Abbot, and with a short walk from the station we were at the racecourse along with, or so it seemed, the world and his wife. Hundreds of people, all of us anticipating a good time, although I wondered how many would be going home poorer than when they arrived. We had set ourselves a strict budget of one modest bet each per race, with any winnings going into the 'pot' towards the Sunday Roast Lunch, booked for the next day at Chappletawton's homely pub.

The whole atmosphere was buzzing with the expectation of excited pleasure; how the trainers and jockeys remained calm I'll never know. The horses were prancing and jogging, tossing their heads and swishing their tails. The crowd watching the parade arena laughed as one of the young jockeys pretended to prance and skitter like his horse was doing. He grinned and waved as he prepared to mount, then set off at a crab-wise canter towards the starting post. Elsie had put her bet on him, and to our delight, he was the winner. His horse was the favourite, though, so I guess that wasn't too much of a surprise, but I did think that the rider of the horse which came second didn't make much of an effort to try to overtake during the last few yards before the winning post. A bit of extra push might just have altered the result.

The left-handed course of just over one mile was oval and almost flat, with seven hurdle-type jumps. For most of the races the horses went round at least twice. Alf said that to win, a jockey needed an agile horse which could pick up the pace approaching the second-to-last fence, as the final run-in was quite short. All of which made each race especially exciting, but I did think that the jockey who came second definitely didn't make much of an exciting attempt to 'pick the pace up'.

(I know, I've used the word 'exciting' a lot – but the whole experience *was* exciting.)

Leaning on the rails by the parade paddock before the second race, Alf noticed someone he knew and waved. The man strolled over to us.

Alf introduced us. "This is Jack Woollen. He owns the training yard down in the valley, Four Horseshoes."

I shook hands enthusiastically. "Laurie's told me a lot about you, Mr Woollen. We saw your stables from the train, and I can see some of the buildings from my bedroom window at Valley View."

"That's right," Jack replied, as enthusiastically. "Equally, I've heard a lot about you, Miss Christopher. Gossip soon gets round in our small community."

He took my hand and kissed it, then did the same to

Elsie and Aunt Madge. All these gallant gentlemen I was meeting; we didn't seem to have them in London.

We were delighted to chat for a short while about the beautiful horses imperiously stalking round the parade ring, their lead ropes held tight by their grooms. Mr Woollen kindly explained the good or poor points of various horses – deep chest, strong bones, pedigree and such; Aunt Madge and I asked general horsey questions, my aunt's being more sensible and useful than mine.

I blushed bright red when I (stupidly) asked, "What happens when a jockey falls off?"

"Protects his head and bits, and hopes a trainer doesn't kick him in the same place for being b-useless," came the immediate answer.

The jockeys trooped out from the weighing room, having changed into the appropriate colours for the different owners they were riding for, and verified that they were carrying the right weight for each race.

Mr Woollen excused himself to join one of them, who didn't seem too happy as he was scowling and shaking his head. I had to look twice, but I was sure that I recognised him. When he mounted Mr Woollen's horse and I got a good look at his face, I was certain. This jockey was the Irishman I had seen in the village arguing with Oliver de Lainé, the one who had pushed past me and was rude. The horrid man who had ignored the trapped deer. I realised, too, that he was the jockey who had come second in the previous race. His name was announced over the Tannoy as Ruairi O'Connor. I was pleased that I'd not chosen his horse to place my modest bet on, despite it being one of Mr Woollen's. And maybe I shouldn't say this, but I was equally as pleased when he came seventh out of eight runners. Judging by Mr Woollen's sour face, the trainer did not, understandably, share my pleasure. The subsequent altercation between the two men as the puffing and sweating horses were led in was also understandable. The jockeys dismounted, unsaddled and headed for the weighing room to have their weight re-confirmed. The horses, their coats steaming, their nostrils flaring, some looking more tired than others, were led away back to the stables by their grooms. For the winner, pats and smiles all round.

The whole thing was exhilarating. The sound of the horses as they had thundered past, the drumming of hooves on what seemed to be hollow ground; the snorting of their hot breath, the clatter of the fences as they skimmed over or through the brush-like 'sticks', and the roared, encouraging cheering of the watching crowd. I could quite see why so many people became hooked on the Sport of Kings, although given that Queen Elizabeth II and the Queen Mother are both passionate about horse racing, I wonder why it is not, now, called the Sport of Queens?

None of us had a win for the third race. My horse came last, but never mind; he wasn't as fast as the others and had tried his best. Perhaps his name, Stroll In The Park, was a giveaway which I should have considered? Mr Woollen's horse, ridden again by O'Connor, was the favourite, but he came in second, losing by a 'head' – the length of the horse's head behind the winner. On principle I hadn't placed a bet on O'Connor as I disliked him. I'm sure he could have tried that extra bit harder to win.

I thought I caught a glimpse of a glum looking Oliver de Lainé among the crowd up in the stands, tearing up a useless betting ticket. Mr Woollen also didn't look happy about losing, but by the parade for the next race he seemed cheerful again.

This race had six runners. I put my bet on Little Lily Lavender because the name sounded fun. Laurie and

Alf teased me because she was an inexperienced outsider and didn't stand a chance against the other runners. Mr Woollen agreed with them. He came over to speak to us again as the horses were walked round the paddock. He kindly invited us to visit his yard any time we liked, which was nice of him, although I had the impression that he enjoyed showing off his equine knowledge to a captive audience. Fair enough for a racehorse trainer I suppose, but he was wrong about Little Lily Lavender!

Racing up towards the second-last fence the favourite, in the lead by a head, wavered and the horse next to him suddenly swerved to the side unseating his jockey, who happened to be O'Connor, which caused the favourite to spook and *his* rider came off as well. At the last fence the new horse in the lead stumbled on landing and he lost valuable time as his rider desperately clung on, managing to wriggle back into the saddle and regather the reins. But it was all too late. Seizing his opportunity, Little Lily Lavender's jockey kicked his horse on in a flying leap over the hurdle, and with arm and whip waving as if there were to be no tomorrow, galloped for the winning post and a well-deserved first place.

Mr Woollen had another runner in the following race. The horse looked stressed and anxious in the parade ring, tossing his head and side-stepping, his coat white-frothed with sweat. Aunt Madge whispered to me that he'd be calmer if his jockey, O'Connor, stopped hauling on the bit and nudging him with his heels – winding the animal up. Hardly anyone placed bets on the horse, guessing, as we had, that he was too unsettled which could severely hamper his performance out on the track. To everyone's surprise, he romped home winning by an easy two lengths. Mr Woollen, I couldn't help noticing, looked extremely smug, pleased to have a winner at last, I supposed. He would not have won anything from betting, as trainers were not allowed to back their own horses, while jockeys were not permitted to bet at all. I guess winning races for the prize money and prestige was even more important for a trainer than winning placed bets. After all, no owner would send his racehorse to be trained by an unsuccessful trainer, would they?

By the final race we were all hoarse (excuse the pun), from cheering our horses on, and we'd managed a win of some sort – had lost as well, but never mind, we were enjoying ourselves. And the final race proved to be another of those 'I don't believe it' moments.

Only four horses were in this last race: two were joint favourites, the third, a promising young horse but with not much experience, and no one was bothering with the fourth, Mr Tivvy, as he was very much a novice. According to the whispers we heard going round, he had been lame for several weeks and was still unfit. Word was that he'd not get round the track even once, let alone twice.

Mr Woollen approached us as we lined up against the paddock rails. He pointed to his own runner, Sovereign Crown, ridden, of course, by Ruairi O'Connor, and whispered that she was a certainty.

"She's my own filly. I've great expectation for her." His praise sounded genuine enough, but I still told Laurie to put my money on Mr Tivvy – as did Aunt Madge *and* Elsie. The three men went with Mr Woollen's filly.

The young horse unseated his rider by slamming on the brakes and stopping at the first fence – the horse, not the rider, who ungracefully sailed over the hurdle without his mount. Coming up to the last hurdle Sovereign Crown was living up to all predictions by being way out in front. She jumped... and O'Connor fell off. I could see no reason why he should be unseated, he just sort of toppled sideways. Frankly, a good rider should have been able to stay on board.

Unbelievably, the horse coming up behind took off wrong, stumbled onto his knees on landing and *his* rider was also unseated. The entire crowd groaned in frustration as that left Mr Tivvy on his own to canter steadily home, puffing and blowing a bit, past the winning post at, hold onto your hats, a stunning 100-1. Tomorrow's birthday treat Sunday lunch was well and truly paid for!

In the unsaddling enclosure, Mr Woollen was busy being angry with O'Connor, who was just as busy being angry back. They weren't shouting but I did, distinctly, hear Mr Woollen say, "You're useless, you were supposed to win."

Well, of course he was! Isn't that the idea of racing? To win?

"It almost makes you think that jockey was deliberately intending to lose," I heard Uncle Toby say to Laurie.

"It probably happens a lot," Laurie answered. "He'll cop it if he's ever rumbled by the Jockey Club, though."

We had intended to say a polite goodbye to Jack Woollen, but left him and his jockey to disagree with each other. I didn't feel sorry for the jockey being on the receiving end of his boss's displeasure. What goes around comes around. He should have helped that deer.

As we were heading back to the train, tired from being on our feet for so long, but happy and much better-off financially than when we had arrived, Laurie noticed Mr de Lainé. He was some way off and looked as fed up as a vulture with toothache, so we thought it best to pretend we hadn't seen him.

7

TAKEN SHORT

We lingered in the town to let the railway crowds thin a bit, found a scrumptious chippy and ate fish and chips wrapped in yesterday's newspaper whilst sitting on a bench in a park near the station, the meal washed down by bottles of Coca Cola for us ladies and beer for the men.

The last part of the journey home by train proved to be amusing, although the men didn't think it was funny. There was no loo on the Tarka Line train, and they had downed several pints of beer at the races, as well as with our meal. Us ladies, sensibly, had visited 'facilities' before catching the train at Exeter. By the time we reached Eggesford where the double line became a single track, Alf, Uncle Toby and Laurie were bursting.

The train always stopped at Eggesford for safety reasons – no driver could proceed on to Barnstaple until he was certain that the train coming *from* Barnstaple had already been and gone. This was ascertained by the collection of a 'key', a token. Basically, if it was not there in the small guard's room then the line was not clear, not safe, so the train could not proceed. Fortunately for our bladder-full menfolk, the train coming from Barnstaple had not yet arrived, which meant that our train had to wait for it. The men quickly nipped out of the stationary carriage to discreetly water the bushes, Aunt Madge standing by the open carriage door to delay a departure if necessary. Men have things much easier when Nature calls don't they? No lowering and raising of undergarments for one thing. In my opinion, pulling tights up in a hurry should be made into an Olympic sport.

At Umberleigh Station, it was rather a squash in Alf's car, all six of us squeezing in where there was really only room for five. Uncle Toby made us laugh by saying, "Just as well there are no policemen about," and pretending to be unable to walk a straight line with one finger pressed against his nose. We reached home in one piece, thankfully. (I'd better add, Elsie drove, not Laurie or Alf.)

Bess was pleased to see us, wagging her tail nineteen to the dozen. Laurie offered to take her for a walk up the lane, and as there was a stunning sunset blooming over to the west, Aunt Madge and I went with him to get a better view from the top of the lane. The three of us leant contentedly on the gate into the meadow watching, fascinated, as the sky beyond the hills turned to salmon pink streaked with shafts of gold, then gradually faded to purple and dark blue. Behind us, a full moon was rising, large and beautiful.

The air was heady with the scent of cut grass, the hay in its neat windrows casting shallow, moon-shadowed patterns across the field. Laurie said that Ralph Greenslade would have turned it some time during the afternoon, explaining that with the gadgets he used attached to the tractor the job was done a lot quicker and easier than before the war, before modern technology came into being.

"All the work would have been done by hand," he explained. "Cut with a scythe, turned over to dry with pitchforks, raked up and bundled into stooks. These would then be tossed onto a cart pulled by a couple of Shire horses or maybe Suffolk Punches or Percherons, and stacked near the farmyard as a neat haystack. I remember Ralph's mother telling me, when I was a young lad, that as they tossed the hay to dry the seeds would fall out along with slugs, beetles and the occasional snake, slow worm or mouse." He laughed. "Most of which, she'd said, went into her hair or down her neck. Thank goodness for modern machinery, eh?"

I shuddered at the thought, and pushed it firmly aside. "This glorious smell would be the same," I said, inhaling deeply but shuddering at the thought of slugs. Ugh, they remind me of leeches. How did people of the past tolerate leeches being purposely put on the skin as a medicinal cure? That scene in *The African Queen* where Charlie – Humphrey Bogart – climbs out of the water and discovers he is covered by the horrible things... makes me shiver just to think about it. I can tolerate most things, but not slugs. Or large, hairy spiders.

Several bats were flitting overhead. Laurie said they were Pipistrelles. I don't know why people are afraid of bats. They are so clever with their athletic ability and precision navigation, swooping and diving after insects that bite us and damage crops and gardens.

Then Aunt Madge spotted a barn owl, shimmering ghostly white beneath the full moon that was rising higher from behind the eastern hedgerow. In awed silence we watched the owl quartering the lines of hay, looking for its supper.

"Their heart-shaped faces are designed to direct

sound to their ears, which are set at slightly different heights in order to pinpoint their prey," Laurie whispered. "Once they've located a mouse, or whatever, they hover overhead then swoop down, grab it with their talons, then eat it whole. Look! There it goes... it's got something. No going hungry tonight."

I thought it not surprising that people of the past – and even today, come to that – thought these incredible birds were ethereal, supernatural spirits. Watching the owl glide silently away across the hedgerows, I could well believe this was a ghost, not a living creature.

8

INTERLUDE - LAURIE

The race day and that evening was the first time I'd seen DCI Christopher truly 'let his hair down' so to speak. He took his job, and all its implications, extremely seriously, but work had been tough these last couple of months; some nasty – really nasty – cases, three of which we'd drawn a blank over, one of them an arson attack resulting in the death of a mother and child. The case was still open, but we were determined to get whoever had callously poured petrol through a front door letterbox, followed by a burning rag. The house had gone up in minutes, with no chance for those inside to escape. It was good for us to get away, put it all behind us for a few days, and hope for fresh evidence to await us when we returned to work.

Bess was pleased to see us as we rolled in after our day out. We had coffee and sat talking in the sitting room as the evening turned to a glorious sunset outside, and I suggested a walk up the lane. Dad and the DCI opted to stay indoors for a last snifter of brandy. Mum was tired; it had been a long day and she was only just over a rotten summer cold, so she went off to bed, leaving Jan, her Aunt Madge, myself and

Bess to enjoy the sunset viewed from up the hill by Top Meadow.

I was content as I strolled back home, hand-in-hand with Jan. Even given the heart-wrenching horrors, the foulness of some criminals and the sheer unpleasantness we often had to face, I loved policework, especially now that I was bagman to DCI Christopher who was everything a policeman *should* be, unlike too many others who abused the position of trust. Corruption, misogyny, racism; there was no place for it within any police force, yet it widely existed. Not within sight nor sound of the DCI though.

The moon was high and bright by the time we got back, bathing everywhere in her silvery-gold sheen, and the barn owl we'd seen had been magical to watch. I hadn't mentioned to the ladies, however, that I'd noticed the beam of a torch down in our woods at the top edge where the stile led into the neighbouring field. I hoped there was an innocent reason, someone walking home from the pub and using the quicker route of the woodland footpath, perhaps? But I feared it could well be poachers after the deer. Venison was a popular, and expensive, meat. Although surely no hunter, legal or otherwise, would be using a torch to see by with such a brilliant moon climbing into the night sky?

Lamping – using lanterns to catch rabbits – was legal, but as far as I was aware no one had sought permission to shoot on our land. And yes, you need permission from the landowner, otherwise you could be accused of trespass and poaching. Not that we had many rabbits in our fields anyway. In the 1950s, myxomatosis, an imported viral disease, had spread to wild rabbits. It had killed millions of the vulnerable animals, spreading rapidly from Kent to Scotland, and to us here in the West Country. Quite a few farmers and foresters welcomed the almost elimination of this agricultural pest. Most people, however, were horrified at seeing thousands of dead and dying conies. Back then, meat was still rationed and hatters and furriers went out of business due to the unavailability of suitable fur. Sir Winston Churchill was personally influential in ensuring that the deliberate transmission of the disease became a criminal offence. That was a long time ago, but the rabbit population still suffered and myxomatosis still killed. Fortunately, the few rabbits we did have on our land appeared to be disease free. I made the sensible decision, however, that whoever was down in our woods could stay there. I wasn't prepared to investigate on my own, not with two very precious ladies present.

Reaching home, Jan and Aunt Madge went indoors to make cocoa. I went on down the lane for a few yards to check that Dad had shut and locked the garage door. It had originally been the smaller of the two old barns on the other side of the lane, opposite the house. Bess came with me, her nose sniffing out all the delightful doggie smells along the hedge, her tail wagging as it always did. I found that the garage padlock was firmly secured and stood a while, looking down across the moonlit valley. The last train to Barnstaple clattered over a bridge, the lights from its carriages winking and blinking as it snaked around the curve of the track, trundled up an incline and was gone from sight, though not sound, as I could hear it chugging and clattering for another couple of minutes.

An owl hooted close by, answered by its mate. Somewhere down in the valley, possibly the training yard at Four Horseshoes, a dog was barking. I mused on how Ruairi O'Connor had fared this evening. Not well I would hazard, for Jack Woollen was not known for mincing his words when disappointed by poor results. Why he employed O'Connor I couldn't fathom. He was not a particularly good rider, let alone a good jockey. Dad had told me that he'd heard rumours that Mr Woollen was not doing as well as he used to – rumours certainly backed up by today's performances. Perhaps he couldn't afford a decent jockey to ride for him now?

There was something more about that jockey that Jan was keeping from me. I'd noticed her grim expression when first seeing him in the parade ring, then her quiet smile of satisfaction when he and his horse had parted company. Had she the same feeling of unease about this guy as I had? That there was something not quite right about his ability and attitude? Or maybe I was imagining things, my policeman's mind working overtime. Seeing shadows where there were none.

I stood, breathing in the damp, night air. I loved Devon, was not keen on London, but then I also loved my job – and that meant London. In London you could not see many stars, too much interference from street lighting, houses, cars, industrial estates. Here, the sky was full of stars, although they were not as brilliant because of the moon. On moonless nights the Milky Way was visible arcing like a distant, misted rainbow – a starbow? – across the back garden. Something bright was fairly low, hovering and twinkling above the hills. The wrong time of year and position for Sirius, the Dog Star. Venus maybe? Too bright for anything else.

Bess nudged my hand as if to tell me she was ready for bed. I put my hand down to fondle her soft, Labrador ears. It had been a good day. I was a lucky man. Kind, supportive parents, a rewarding, mostly enjoyable job, and a beautiful young woman who would, soon, be my wife. I couldn't believe my luck that I had found Jan, although I did occasionally wonder what on earth she saw in me, an ordinary, nothing special guy. Yes, I was a policeman, but that didn't make me Batman or Superman, did it?

The dog down in the valley had stopped barking. Apart from the wind rustling through the trees, all was quiet. Tomorrow – I had a quick look at my watch, no, today – was Mum's birthday. Nothing special, she was forty-something, (I'll not be indelicate enough to reveal a lady's age), but whatever her age she was special to me and Dad, and, I hoped, Jan also.

One last glance at the sky and a shooting star flared across the heavens. I made a wish, and no, I'll not reveal that, either.

Tucked up in bed, I took a while to fall asleep. Partly because Jan was at the other end of the house, alone in *her* bed and I rather wished we could be together, but discretion meant otherwise, and partly, I couldn't sleep because my mind wouldn't let go of that torchlight in the woods. I must have succumbed at some point, though, because I awoke muzzily, with a vague, early morning mist-bound greyness beyond the window, and Bess downstairs, barking.

I groaned and was tempted to bury my head under the pillow, but the barking continued, and I realised that someone was frantically knocking at our front door.

9

A BODY? WHAT BODY?

We were all awake. Alf and Laurie ran down the stairs while the rest of us peered over the banisters, wondering who on earth could be bashing at the door at five-thirty in the morning. In the hall, Alf grabbed the still barking Bess's collar and Laurie opened the door. A woman half-staggered, half-fell into his arms.

"That's Dorothy Clack!" Elsie exclaimed as she tightened her dressing gown belt and hurried down the stairs.

I was surprised. I'd somehow assumed that Mrs Dorothy Clack was a frail, grey-haired old biddy, but she was neither frail nor old; in fact she was about Elsie's age and the almost spitting image of popular shop worker, Mavis Wilton, in the television series *Coronation Street*, played by actress Thelma Barlow. The character was a moralising, dithering spinster with a fertile imagination. The sort of woman who had no idea how to arrange her paranoid soul, just like Mrs Clack.

"Oh crikey," I whispered to Aunt Madge and Uncle Toby as we trailed more sedately in Elsie's wake, "I hope it's not another flying saucer or walkabout scarecrow hoax, not at this unearthly time of the morning!"

Elsie managed to prise Mrs Clack's clutching hands away from Laurie's dressing gown collar – the woman was nearly strangling him in her deep distress. "Come into the kitchen and sit down, pet," Elsie said. "What about a nip of brandy, Alfred?"

Mrs Clack's pale face wrinkled into disapproval. "No, no, I never touch alcohol."

"I'll put the kettle on," Aunt Madge offered as an alternative shock remedy. "I reckon we could all do with a cup of tea."

"No time for that! Oh dear, oh dear. I didn't know what to do!" The distraught woman pulled away from Elsie and shifted her clinging fingers to Alf. "He's dead! Down in the woods! He's dead!"

Laurie helped steer Mrs Clack into the kitchen and sat her down. We gathered round, concerned and puzzled.

"Who is dead, Dorothy?" Elsie asked, taking the woman's hands in her own. Poor Mrs Clack was in such a state; her dress was torn, her hair was dangling in disarray from what had, I assumed, been a neat chignon not long ago. Her coat was half off and she had bramble scratches on her legs and hands.

"Or *what* is dead, Mrs Clack?" Laurie added, squatting down in front of her. "Have you found a dead badger or deer, perhaps? I think there might have been poachers around last night."

She grasped his hand and I saw Laurie wince, she held it so tight. "I watch that big sett of badgers at the back of your field most nights. I make myself comfortable in a little camouflaged den I've made amongst those rhododendron bushes and sit and watch them until dawn. I take scraps of food for them. They're quite tame now. Did you know that badgers love peanuts? I buy them especially."

"Yes, I knew that. So, you were in the woods, watching the badgers? What time was this?"

"I go down there about midnight."

"With a torch?"

I thought that was a rather odd question for Laurie to ask her, but didn't comment. He would, no doubt, have his reasons.

Mrs Clack produced a torch from her coat pocket. "Yes, of course. You'd not expect me to walk through the woods without one, would you?"

Laurie smiled, explained. "No, I thought I saw torchlight last night, wondered if it was poachers, but it was probably you, which is a relief. Do go on, Mrs Clack, what happened next?"

"I was making my way home and found him."

"Him?"

"The leprechaun. He was slumped against the headstone. Quite dead."

Laurie raised an eyebrow as he looked up at my uncle, who quietly put a hand on his shoulder and nodded at some unspoken mutual agreement.

"Mr Christopher here is a police Detective Chief Inspector. We'll get dressed and go and look," Laurie said with a calming smile. "You stay here, Mrs Clack, and have a nice cup of tea."

"I'll come with you," Alf offered.

The three men disappeared upstairs to dress, Mrs Clack saying that she knew Laurie was here, and that he was a policeman. "It was nearer to come here than go all the way back to the village. I got caught in the brambles. Oh dear, look at my dress; I'll never be able to mend these tears." Forlornly she showed us the jagged rip along the hem. A solitary tear trickled down her cheek. She was shaking, from shock, I guessed. I knew myself how distressing it can be to find a dead body.

Aunt Madge handed her a cup of hot, sweet tea and poured for Elsie and me as well. I'd noticed that Aunt Madge had discreetly slipped a drop of Elsie's cooking brandy into Mrs Clack's tea.

Uncle Toby and Laurie returned, having hurriedly dressed.

Mrs Clack managed a weak smile; the tea was helping her to calm down. "I adore watching the badgers. That big sett has two cubs. But when I got to the clearing..." her voice trailed off into a gulp and another tear slid down her cheek.

"We'll go and see what's there, don't worry," Laurie reassured her, and headed for the back door with Uncle Toby and Alf. Bess was up for going as well, but she was firmly told to 'stay'.

They were gone for about an hour. We'd moved into the sitting room where it was more comfortable. Mrs Clack had very soon fallen asleep on the settee, her mouth open and snoring softly, while Elsie, Aunt Madge and I took it in turns to go upstairs to wash and dress. It was still early, but there was no point in going back to bed; all the same, I think we also dozed off because Bess barking woke us all with a start.

Laurie and Uncle Toby walked in, both looking grim. Laurie went to sit next to Mrs Clack, who, rousing, seemed disorientated. Aunt Madge was about to say something to Uncle Toby, but he shook his head and put one finger to his lips. I guessed that he was leaving this to Laurie because Mrs Clack knew him.

"Now then, Dorothy. Is it all right if I call you Dorothy?" Laurie asked, gently.

She nodded.

"Tell us exactly what you saw and found."

Mrs Clack looked a bit puzzled, but managed to tell her story again. "I was heading home after watching the badgers. I entered the clearing and saw him, lying against Avril's headstone."

"Did you see or hear anyone else in the woods?" Uncle Toby asked.

Mrs Clack shook her head. "All I saw were the badgers and the dead leprechaun."

"And how did you know he was dead, Dorothy? Did you touch him?"

She looked horrified at Laurie's suggestion. "I did not! I'd not dare to touch a leprechaun, alive or dead! I knew he was dead because he looked dead. His eyes were open, but he wasn't moving or breathing."

Laurie raised his eyebrows and formed a patient sort of look.

Uncle Toby squatted down in front of Dorothy. "Mrs Clack, we found nothing there in the clearing. Beyond trampled grass, there was no sign of a body. All we found was this..." He beckoned to Alf, who came forward and showed us an empty whisky bottle wrapped in a handkerchief to preserve any fingerprints.

"This wasn't there on Friday, when I was in the clearing with Jan," Laurie said, "so, I'm afraid it's more likely that what you saw, Dorothy, was a very drunk man. He was dead *drunk*, not dead. You must have disturbed him somehow, for he is not there now."

Alf added, "I expect he's staggered home, with a very sore head that he'll regret later."

Dorothy Clack was shaking her head. "No, no, I expect the Irish angels took him. Oh!" She put her hand to her mouth. "Oh, if I had stayed, I would have seen them."

Laurie ignored that, asked, patiently, "Why do you think he was a leprechaun, Dorothy?"

She became a little tetchy at that.

"Young man, I know a leprechaun when I see one. He is little, wears a green jacket and I have heard his Irish accent. So, what else could he be?"

10

BACON FOR BREAKFAST, BEEF FOR LUNCH

Alf took Dorothy home in the car. I could see, now, why Heather in the village shop called her 'Dotty' for she was as mad as a hatter. Not one of us had dared to ask her why there would be an *Irish* leprechaun in a *Devonshire* wood because the question was so silly it didn't occur to us to ask, not until Alf returned and we were sitting around the kitchen table devouring the bacon sandwiches Elsie and Aunt Madge were making. The kitchen was deliciously filled with the smell of frying bacon and fresh-made, percolated coffee.

"Heather was passing by, taking her dog for its morning walk – I'm glad we have the advantage of a door straight onto a garden. Heather's flat above the shop has a back garden the size of a postage stamp. Anyway, she saw me dropping Mrs Clack off, and wanted to know what was going on," Alf told us through a mouthful of doorstop-sized bread slices filled with crisp bacon. "I would have kept quiet, but Mrs C promptly told her all about this woodland leprechaun. The nonsense will be spread all round the village by midday, and then she started complaining that there was a scarecrow in the telephone box. She insisted that I look. Nothing there, of course."

"I expect Mrs Clack thinks that Irish jockey of Mr Woollen's is the leprechaun." I said, thoughtfully licking HP brown sauce from my fingers. (Why does brown and tomato sauce from sandwiches, or jam from doughnuts always drip everywhere?)

Laurie frowned, confused, then laughed. "Of course! A short man, wearing a green jacket and talking with an Irish accent!"

"I've not seen him in the village," Elsie said, "and Mrs Clack certainly doesn't go to the races."

"But we know that he *has* been in the village, and that he uses the footpath through the woods..." I broke off, realised that I hadn't told Laurie about my brief encounter in the village on Friday afternoon. I quickly related that I had seen the Irishman arguing with Oliver de Lainé, and that having bumped into me, and been rude, he'd stormed off down the path through the woods in the direction of Four Horseshoes. I didn't add anything about the deer, as I wasn't sure if the encounter would upset Elsie; Laurie and I had deliberately kept that incident to ourselves, although he had quietly spoken to Alf, who promised to sort the fence out as soon as he got the chance.

I did say, however, "We know that Mrs Clack is often in the woods, as she told Heather that she'd seen a leprechaun there, so..." I tailed off again, certain that two and two were making four. "And those cigarette butts you picked up, Laurie, were possibly his."

"Slightly circumstantial, Cupcake," Uncle Toby said. Laurie agreed, but conceded that I might be onto something.

I wasn't going to argue with either of them. The owner of the discarded cigarette butts *was* only conjecture, but I *knew* I was right about the identity of Dorothy Clack's leprechaun.

"Why would he be hanging around in the woods?" Elsie asked.

"To meet someone, perhaps?" Aunt Madge ventured.

"And I think I can guess who and why," Laurie stated. "Jockeys are not allowed to bet on any horses in any races. If they want something quiet on the side, they have to be very circumspect about it."

"And get someone to place bets for them!" I crowed. I clapped my hands together in triumph, added, "He meets Mr Oliver de Lainé in the secrecy of the woods, that's what the argument was about. De Lainé doesn't want to be seen with O'Connor!"

"Well, even if Oliver de Lainé *is* placing illegal bets, it's nothing to do with us. And if O'Connor *is* this jockey, he *isn't* a leprechaun, and there isn't a dead body, so let's set all this aside as we're forgetting something far more important," Alf proclaimed. He raised his cup of coffee and proposed a toast. "To my dear wife. Happy birthday!"

"Happy birthday!" we responded, raising our own cups. Elsie opened some birthday cards, but said she'd like to have her presents later, to make the day last longer.

Naturally, Laurie joked, "Oh, do you expect presents, then Mum?" We laughed again. Of course she had presents! I had a newly published book by one of her favourite authors, and Laurie had a gorgeous silk scarf for her.

"What was that about the scarecrow, Dad?" Laurie asked, helping himself to yet another cup of coffee.

"What? Oh, she was complaining that yesterday afternoon there'd been a scarecrow sitting on the bench by the village pond. Then last night, on her way to the woods, she'd seen it *inside* the phone box. She's adamant that the thing is following her about."

"Someone playing tricks, I expect," Elsie said. "She does rather leave herself open to pranks."

I glanced at the kitchen clock. It was only just gone 9 a.m. We'd been up for hours! I'm not sure if it was that fact, or feeling appreciatively full of bacon butties that caused it, but we migrated to the sitting room, sprawled in the comfortable chairs and one by one, we fell asleep. Even Bess, I noticed before I too dozed, was stretched out on a rug, snoring.

The snooze did us good, and by midday we were ready to tidy ourselves and head up the hill to the village pub, where Alf had booked a table for a Sunday Roast Lunch.

The Exeter Inn is a long way from Exeter, which is in the south of Devon; Chappletawton is in the north. Not many people realise that Devon is England's third largest county and is unique because it is the only one with two separate coastlines. When the inn was built during Queen Elizabeth I's long reign, it was the first stopping point for coaches travelling from Barnstaple to Exeter – hence its name. Here, the tired horses would be changed and passengers could take a quick, essential break. The inn (or pub as locals now tend to call it) has a thatched roof topped with a fox stalking two pheasants, while inside is a comfortable bar and lounge, perfect for a quiet drink or a splendid meal. I had met Hazel and Steve, who ran the Exeter, at Christmas and it was lovely to be welcomed back as if I were a regular local. Despite it only being soon after opening, the place was busy, most people seated outside at wooden picnic benches enjoying the sunshine and a ploughman's lunch.

Inside, we found Oliver de Lainé, who greeted us enthusiastically by raising his pint glass of locally brewed cider, before politely getting to his feet, and referring to our previous Shakespearean conversation, declared, "If it isn't my fair Juliet and her handsome Romeo, come, I perceive, with the families Capulet and Montague?"

Laurie laughed as he indicated Uncle Toby and Aunt Madge. "We are hardly feuding families, Mr de Lainé. Meet my future in-laws."

Hands were shaken, although did I perceive a slight hesitation on Mr de Lainé's part when Laurie introduced Uncle Toby as Detective Chief Inspector Christopher? It was not unusual for people to pause when they discovered my uncle's profession. I'd probably meet the same reaction when introducing Laurie to my friends as a detective sergeant. Was this common uncertainty caused by a guilty conscience in people, I wonder?

If it was a twinge of guilt at some black secret, placing illegal bets, for instance, Oliver de Lainé swiftly set it aside. To me, taking my hand and kissing it, he said, "How delightful to see you again, my dear Miss Christopher. And Mrs Walker, how charming you look today!" He then enthused over Aunt Madge, who (and no disrespect to Elsie) was by far the most glamorous of the three of us.

Ralph Greenslade and his two sons, Kevin and Doug, were enjoying pints of beer, Ralph saying they'd popped in for a quick drink to get out from under Mrs Greenslade's feet while she prepared their Sunday roast.

"I'll be up t'turn hay agin dreckly after I've eaten," Ralph announced in his Devon accent, as he headed for the door. "The tedder's rowed it nicely. It should be jus' right fer balin' t'morrow I as reckon, if'n the weather 'olds. C'mon you two lads, let's be 'avin' thee." The young men finished their beers, wished

Elsie a happy birthday, and bidding everyone a general goodbye, left.

Steve, behind the bar, asked what we all wanted to drink.

I preferred white wine, so asked for that. "What's a tedder?" I whispered to Laurie, having never heard the word before.

"The tedder – or haybob, same machine but fitted slightly differently – is a machine attached to the tractor. It lifts and separates the cut hay in order to hasten drying time by improving the air flow through the windrow, and brings the lower layer up to the top."

Steve placed glasses of wine for me, Elsie and Aunt Madge on the bar. "I hear you had a visitor early this morning?" he said as he pulled pints of beer for Laurie, Alf and Uncle Toby. "Dotty Dorothy seeing her fairy tale characters again, was she?"

Alf laughed, and had to move away from the doorway as someone else came in.

"Fairy tales?" the newcomer enquired, "I could do with a fairy godmother to magic up a reliable jockey, if you happen to know of one?"

Alf beamed at Jack Woollen and filled him in with what had been happening. "It seems that Dorothy Clack has been seeing fairy people. Says she found a dead leprechaun in the woods early this morning. Of course, we went to look but there was nothing there – which was to be expected. As he's the only Irishman around, we assume she'd come across your jockey the worse for wear from drink, and by the time she'd fetched us he'd come round and staggered off in a homeward direction."

Mr Woollen frowned. "He's not in his flat above my office. I checked because he didn't turn up to exercise the horses this morning. I'm not paying him for work he doesn't do." He snorted mild laughter, asked,

"Dorothy Clack? Is she the woman who lives in the first cottage? Always coming up with fanciful tales?"

"That's the one. It was flying saucers a short while ago."

Mr Woollen nodded, then frowned again. "Bit of a coincidence, though. I only came in to see if O'Connor was here, drowning his sorrows. I told him yesterday that if he ever rode as badly again, I'd sack him. I wondered if I might find him propping up a bar somewhere. I've tried the Plymouth Arms and the Rising Moon, his usual haunts. But as no one there's seen him, I thought I'd try further afield. The man's a useless drunk. He will have to go. Has he been in at all, Steve?"

Behind the bar, Steve shook his head. "Not since Friday. He came in just after opening at 5.30 looking for Mr de Lainé. Had a face like thunder. Did he find you, Oliver?"

We automatically turned to where Oliver de Lainé had been seated, only to find his chair unoccupied and his glass of cider on the table, abandoned. A torn, red and orange matchbook was in the ashtray, along with several cigarette butts and used matches.

"Probably visiting the gents," Steve said. "What'll you have, Jack?"

"No thanks, can't stop, got stables to do, horses to see to, and I'm a man down." To us, asked, "I hope you all had a more productive day at Newton Abbot than I did? Why not come down for evening stables later, have a look round? We're usually pretty quiet on a Sunday, and maybe my missing jockey will have turned up by then."

Hazel, with her bright, cheery smile, came to tell us that our table was ready. It had been laid especially for Elsie, with colourful balloons tied to the back of her chair, and more birthday cards from people in the village piled at her place setting.

We forgot about Dotty Dorothy, leprechauns and jockeys when Sunday lunch was served: traditional roast beef, fluffy Yorkshire Pudding, crisp roast potatoes and a selection of fresh vegetables. By the time we'd also enjoyed a Hazel-made dessert of apple crumble and custard, we were as stuffed as marrows. The men opted to prop up the bar for a final brandy, while we savoured rich Irish coffee topped with a thick layer of cream, accompanied by wafer-thin chocolate mints. Needless to say, I had completely abandoned any consideration for my waistline.

In no hurry to go home, we sat chatting to a couple of ladies at the next table, then thanked Hazel for her culinary skills and excellent hospitality. We were distracted, though, by something occurring at the bar.

Ralph Greenslade had hurried in and appeared to be in a state of great agitation. Uncle Toby and Laurie were going out the door. As we approached the bar, Steve was offering Mr Greenslade a tot of brandy.

"What's happened?" I asked, recognising the unmistakable signs of something seriously wrong.

Ralph downed the brandy in one gulp. His hands were shaking.

"There be a body in the meadow," he gasped. "Buried 'neath the hay."

11

INTERLUDE - LAURIE

DCI Christopher squatted beside the very dead corpse, puffed his cheeks and with one finger, tipped his hat back slightly.

"I'd normally bawl someone out for moving a body at a crime scene," he said, momentarily resting both hands on his grey-trousered knees. Together, we had rolled the corpse over so that we could see the face, and I'd identified him as Ruairi O'Connor, the jockey. He'd been strangled with a length of baling twine, found almost everywhere in the West Country and beyond.

It was doubtful that he'd been strangled here, in the lower corner of my father's meadow where the hay lay in neat rows. Ralph, as he'd promised, had turned most of it again with the haybob which resembled a pair of whirligig rakes that spun round at high speed in order to 'fluff it up' – my layman's non-agricultural term. Turning in this way ensured the hay was properly dry, and also shook any seeds of grass and wildflowers back onto the ground. Ralph would later graze his cattle and sheep up here, their hooves squishing the seeds deeper into the earth ready for regrowth next year, enhanced by the spread of natural fertiliser –

animal dung. I've often thought that the world must have been knee deep in dung back in the days of the dinosaurs. They were enormous creatures that must have left behind a vast amount of excrement. I suspect that's why huge areas of land now have acres and acres of fertile soil.

DCI Christopher was making a quick search through the dead jockey's pockets. "Wouldn't normally advocate doing this," he muttered grimly, "but given the circumstances..."

I knew what he meant. Too many policemen, of whatever rank, were never careful or considerate of preserving a crime scene before forensics arrived. My boss was one of the rare, meticulous coppers who took his job seriously and – usually – did things by the book.

Using his handkerchief, rather than touch items and leave fingerprints, he found a packet of Woodbines and a matchbook in one jacket pocket.

"Oliver de Lainé seems to have the same brand," I observed, indicating the distinctively patterned matchbook. "Red and orange, and is that the Statue of Liberty behind the print? An American brand?"

DCI Christopher squinted at the matchbook. "Looks like it. Doesn't mean de Lainé was here, though."

"No, but it does prove he knows O'Connor and has met up with him." I had a thought, suppressed a laugh, pointed at the Woodbines. "Wasn't the manufacturer's advertisement something like, '*Light up life with a Woodbine*'? Didn't light up much life for this poor blighter, did they?"

"At least he won't die from lungs full of poisoning tar."

I snorted grim amusement at the gallows humour. It's not that we're ghouls or unfeelingly crass, but dark humour helps us cope with the dreadful things that we all too often have to deal with. It's a way of helping to sort our minds around what is, or isn't, important.

In another pocket, a plastic wallet containing his Jockey Club membership ID and two one-pound notes. Nothing else. I glanced at the tractor and its haybob parked up at the top of the field; on finding the body, Ralph had abandoned his work and driven to the village to summon help. He stood, now, a few feet away from us looking, I must say, a little green around the gills.

"'Twere only luck I saw 'im," he said, seeing my glance in his direction. "I were comin' down next row along…" he pointed at where the hay had been freshly turned, "… an' saw a foot sticking out." He wiped his damp face with one hand, the sweat from the heat of the day and his own unsettled alarm beading on his forehead. "I thought as sommun were asleep or playin' a daft trick by 'idin' a boot there. I almost ignored it an' carried on…" He gulped and, grim faced at the thought, turned away. I don't think any of us were keen to dwell on the unpleasant consequences of a human corpse meeting with a tractor and its attached machinery.

"I'd say he's been here some while. Dead for a good few hours. No sign of a struggle – no trampled grass or kicked-about hay," DCI Christopher said as he got slowly to his feet. "And we know that he wasn't killed here, but in that clearing – unless whoever moved him to here, to hide the body, strangled him somewhere else and then propped him up against that gravestone."

I chewed my lip in thought. "Unless," I hesitated, "unless Dorothy Clack was not telling us the truth?"

DCI Christopher pulled a sceptical face. "She strangled him, hid him, then came to set us on a wild goose chase? Is that likely?"

I shook my head. It wasn't.

"It's more plausible that she's telling us exactly

what she saw. O'Connor either secretively came to the clearing to meet someone, or came *with* someone, during the night, assuming they would be unobserved."

"Someone he then fell out with over something?" I answered, looking around for any further corroborating clues.

"There are clear tracks here," Ralph Greenslade said, pointing to two lines of scuffed marks on the dusty, sun-baked soil. "Made from where he's been dragged into the field from the woods, perhaps?"

I inspected O'Connor's boots. Mr Greenslade's deduction was confirmed by new scratches and scuffs on the heels of the victim's leather boots.

My boss thrust his hands into his jacket pockets as he glanced around, taking in details, looking for oddities that could be obscure clues. "*Mmm hmm.* Dragged from the clearing, covered by the hay. But why? Why move him? Why hide him? From respect for the dead or to optimise a chance to get away?"

"The latter, I suspect." I answered. "Someone who murders someone by strangling them isn't likely to have much respect."

DCI Christopher shrugged. "You'd be surprised, but hiding evidence to make the crime disappear, ostrich in the sand syndrome, is common. Remorse, fear, panic? A lot depends on whether a murder is planned or spur of the moment anger or fear. The consequences can affect different people in different ways."

I thought about that for a moment. He was right. The next question, though, was motive. Was this a planned revenge of some sort, or an impromptu reaction to a quarrel or disappointment? Was the murder connected to racing or money – to betting? Or could it be sex, greed, jealousy?

This was a frustrating situation. Neither of us, despite being the police, could do much more than observe and speculate; this was not our patch, would not be our case. Initial response would come from South Molton Constabulary, then a DS and DI would arrive from Barnstaple. I hoped DS Frobisher would not be the one to be called out, I knew him of old, and knew him to be lazy, inefficient, rude and everything a police detective shouldn't be.

"It looks like Dorothy Clack was right," I said with a heavy sigh. "She *did* find a dead leprechaun."

DCI Christopher nodded. "That she did, but did she see anything or anyone else? Did the killer realise that he was not alone in these woods? Mrs Clack was well hidden, busy badger watching. She says that she didn't see or hear anything untoward – but how could a murderer be certain of that? If this were my case, I'd be up there talking to her now. And keeping a WPC close by for her safety. Once it gets out that she was here in these woods, a possible witness, she could be in danger. Or is whoever strangled this poor chap aware of her frequent telling of fantasy tales? Did he see her find the body, watch her trot away to summon help, then attempt to hide the evidence, guessing she would not be believed? The old cry wolf syndrome. Say some sort of nonsense often enough, and people stop listening. Which is exactly what we did. We didn't believe her." He trailed off, not needing to say more.

"That means whoever did this is local," I concluded. "Someone well known round the village, and who knows her reputation."

DCI Christopher nodded solemnly. "Agreed."

"Narrows it down to about three-hundred people," Ralph Greenslade ventured.

I said, "A jockey, murdered in the woods after a disagreement of some sort. Racing related, maybe? It wouldn't surprise me, after that poor performance yesterday, that someone was disgruntled enough to lose his temper. Jan told me that, when he fell off, any half-decent rider should have been capable of staying aboard his horse. Or was the body propped against the old headstone as a macabre message to someone? A warning? To Jack Woollen? That's his cousin's headstone, after all. The immediate intention was to leave O'Connor there, but Mrs Clack unexpectedly appeared. She ran off, hysterical, and he has to think quick, buy himself some time to create plausible alibis."

DCI Christopher pursed his lips, deep in his own thoughts. "Possibly, probably, though it must have taken a good few minutes to move him. Why not leave him where he was and take that time to clear off? We were here in about forty minutes? Forty-five?"

I didn't agree with that. "Ah, but whoever did this might not have expected Dorothy to come direct to our house. Logically, she'd have gone back to the village, called the police from there. By the time anyone actually came it could be closer to, what, not far off two hours?"

A police car pulled into the field, parked by the gate. Two coppers got out and putting their hats on, strolled down the hill towards us. From here on, whatever the speculation, beyond the giving of our own detailed statements, any observations, conjecture or theories – and the eventual outcome – would be nothing to do with us.

12

"PUT THE KETTLE ON"

As Laurie had feared, Barnstaple sent DS Frobisher to investigate an allegation of murder. When the original constables from South Molton had arrived, Laurie and Uncle Toby didn't wait in the meadow as there was no point in hanging around or inadvertently getting in the way, so they'd left word of their whereabouts and come back to Valley View. Two hours later, Mr Greenslade joined us. He had gone home – there had been stock to check and feed, farm work to do – and he was furious. He'd gone to the meadow to see about retrieving his tractor, but had been told to leave it in situ, 'in case'. In case of what, no one had explained. The two constables had connections to farming folk and had known to park their car at the top of the field. DS Frobisher had not, either deliberately or unintentionally, taken note of farming protocol. As Mr Greenslade had discovered, the DS had eventually arrived and driven across the field, disregarding the fact that his car was crushing the cut hay, and that the bumpy, uneven ground was not good for his suspension.

I'd had the misfortune of meeting him at Christmas.

Naturally, I knew quite a few policemen who were based in or around Chingford, some I knew well, some as mere acquaintances with our paths only crossing at police social functions or on the occasions when I visited the police canteen. Most were respectful because of who my uncle was; a few I deliberately avoided. Frobisher, based here in Devon, would firmly come into that last category. He was arrogant and patronising, a thoroughly nasty man. My consolation: Laurie also disliked him.

The first thing DS Frobisher said to me when I answered the front door at Valley View was, "Put the kettle on, love. Two sugars," followed by a smirking look at my tee-shirt which, although not low cut, was enough to show my 'assets' (which were not all that wonderful, to be honest, just averagely ordinary), and then gave a hefty pat on my bottom. I glared at him and moved aside.

Aunt Madge had followed me into the hall. She looked him up and down contemptuously. "I strongly advise you to keep your inappropriate hands to yourself, young man. And are jeans suitable apparel for an officer of the law?"

"It's supposed to be my day off. Technically, I'm off-duty, ma'am." He further blotted his copybook by saying 'ma'am' to rhyme with 'farm', a mispronunciation which always irked Aunt Madge. She is by no means a snob, but does not suffer fools, especially extremely rude ones.

Imperiously, she reprimanded him. "Off duty you might have been, but you are *on* duty now, and should dress accordingly. And it is ma'am as in 'jam' not 'marm' as in 'farm.' Although police and military officers often seem to think otherwise. In addition, my niece is not a housemaid, so you will conduct your business without the necessity of refreshment." Surreptitiously, she winked at me.

For a few seconds Frobisher stood silent, his mouth opening and closing like a stranded herring, with no idea how to respond. Luckily for him, Laurie appeared. I disliked Frobisher, but I did feel sorry for him – for a few seconds. Being on the sharp end of Aunt Madge's tongue is not for the faint hearted. Once he had gone into the sitting room with Laurie, to where Uncle Toby and Ralph Greenslade were waiting, I caught Aunt Madge's eye and we burst into laughter.

"Being semi-posh," she chuckled, "has its uses on occasion."

DS Frobisher left after about forty-five minutes, his tail tucked firmly between his legs having been stoutly reprimanded by Mr Greenslade for not taking due care of his hay crop, by Uncle Toby for not listening attentively enough to the detailed statements made by experienced policemen, and soundly advised by Laurie to interview Mrs Clack with a gloved hand. I didn't think Frobisher's demeanour lasted further than the garden gate, however, for he sped away up the lane with a resounding squeal of tyres. I hoped he wouldn't meet any obstacles – straying sheep or a tractor. For their sake, not his.

I was not, as Aunt Madge had said, the housemaid but I put the kettle on for a cup of tea because I thought we deserved one now that awful man had gone. Elsie had taken herself upstairs for a rest straight after we'd returned from lunch; I'd promised her a cuppa at about four-thirty, and it was now past that.

Poor Elsie was, quite rightly, upset by the turn of the day's events. Such a shame because it had been a wonderful meal at the pub, but after a slight discussion we agreed that we should take up Mr Woollen's offer to visit his training yard to compensate and finish the day off nicely. We weren't being heartless, but Laurie and Uncle Toby were on leave, the murder was not their case and we thought it better for them both to stay firmly out of the way. And to leave everything to the obnoxious DS Frobisher. Even if he wasn't all that competent.

13

THROUGH THE LENS

Leaning on a wooden gate, watching thoroughbred mares with foals at foot contentedly grazing on a beautiful summer evening was my idea of heaven. The early evening had cooled down from the day's heat, aided by a gentle westerly breeze that had sprung up and was riffling through the surrounding trees. The mares, cropping grass and swishing tails to ward off annoying flies created a calmness to what had, unfortunately, partially been an unpleasant day. Watching the foals kicking up their heels drove away those troublesome events. Had I known the dead jockey, O'Connor, personally, and had he been a nicer person, my thoughts might have been more compassionate, but as it was, this idyllic scene that I was surveying with the people I loved prevented any encroachment of compassionate conscience.

"I like that chestnut foal," Aunt Madge said, pointing out a cheeky filly who was goading her dam to come and play. Sensible mum was ignoring her daughter, the grass holding more attraction. Aunt Madge focused her camera and took several more pictures; I reckoned that she had already used up most of the reel of film. The long-legged foals were several months old and rapidly gaining in size and strength. Thoroughbred racehorses have an official birthday, regardless of when they are actually born, therefore, the youngsters enjoying the evening sunshine would all be one year old on January 1st next year. That was all right for the early-borns, but a disadvantage for anything arriving towards the middle or later in the year – a foal born in late July, for instance, would be classed as a yearling in the following January, despite only being six months old.

"You might like her," Uncle Toby cautioned, "but we are not buying her."

Aunt Madge snorted. "What would I be wanting a racehorse for?"

"To raise and train as a showjumper, perhaps?" I teased, which was unfair of me, as my aunt already had two fabulous horses, but neither of them were particularly good jumpers and I knew that jumping was what Aunt Madge had dreams of doing. Even popping over a fallen log measuring less than a baked bean tin in height was too big for me. The thought of the enormous showjumps that the professionals such as David Broome and Harvey Smith flew over as if their horses were a winged Pegasus, scared me witless.

"Showjumping is a very different kind of jumping to how we train our horses," Mr Woollen said. "For racing they need to jump long and low; it doesn't matter if their feet brush through the hurdles, the idea is to reach the winning post first, not jump a clear round. Creating a perfect arc shape over a fence can lose valuable seconds when racing."

"The skill in showjumping," Aunt Madge replied, "is, as you say, to get round a course without incurring faults by knocking poles down or putting in a stop."

"And to jump clear and fast in a jump-off against the clock?" Alf asked.

"Yes, and that takes skill as well, to know where to cut in or lengthen a stride, increase, decrease pace. It isn't just a case of pointing the horse at a jump and hoping for the best."

"I'd not like to jump anything at the speeds racehorses go at," I declared. "A nice, steady canter on the flat is fine for me."

"Ah, but to gallop with the power and speed of a horse beneath you, the wind in your face... nothing can beat that exhilaration. Nothing!" Mr Woollen pushed away from the gate and beckoned us back towards the yards and stables. "Come on, I'll show you my two stallions. They've been winners in their day, of more value now for breeding rather than risk them racing, although we don't do a lot of stud breeding here, I like to have these few mares around. Our priority is the training and actual racing."

He was being a most gracious and informative host, and didn't seem that bothered about losing his resident jockey, although I suspect he was partly relieved to be rid of him, as well as being tactful by not mentioning the subject. All he had said was that the police had come to speak to him, but he'd not seen O'Connor since yesterday evening, when he'd gone off in a huff having been threatened with the sack.

"They asked me outright if I'd killed him," Mr Woollen had said indignantly to us. "Why would I? Apart from him being a lousy, lazy, rider what motive would I have had? Easier to simply sack the no-good idiot. Killing him would be akin to hacking someone's head off in order to cure a sore throat!"

We followed him from the fields to the stables. There were three separate yards, one for the mares, one for the young horses and those in training, and the two stallions had their own stables a short distance away across a fenced, sand-school exercise manège. I couldn't help noticing, however, that quite a few of the stables were empty. Perhaps their occupants were all out at grass in fields further away?

Mr Woollen showed us round, stopping to tell us about his favourite or special horses, giving them titbits of sliced carrots from what appeared to be a bottomless pocket, and explaining the training routines for getting his horses fit. We could clearly see how carefully looked after they were; after all, these were the precious athletes of the horse world, maybe even a potential Cheltenham Gold Cup or even a Grand National winner was amongst them.

Three stable lads and two girls were completing the evening rounds, hanging up haynets for the horses, cleaning their bedding of wet straw and droppings, making ready for the night to come. In the last, main yard, a few of the horses were banging on their stable doors with their hooves, demanding dinner to be served – Aunt Madge's were the same, greedy and impatient. I thought it rather harsh, however, when Mr Woollen snapped at one of the stable girls to get a move on. She was very petite and struggling with a capacity-filled haynet that was almost half her size and weight – I knew from experience how heavy haynets could be. Rather than shout at her, I thought Mr Woollen could have offered to help, but then, I suppose the girl was being paid to do a job. I did notice that she scowled at him behind his back. I can't say that I blamed her.

The yard itself was tidy and attractive. White-washed walls, door and window frames painted dark, forest green, colourful hanging baskets of red, white and pink geraniums dotted here and there. It all looked welcoming, but I couldn't help thinking that this was the public area; what was it like 'behind the scenes', as it were?

A green-painted wooden bench was set against the wall of what looked, at a quick glance through the window, to be the yard's office, above which was a small flat, judging by the colourful curtains at the three windows. I suspected that it might have been converted from what, in olden days, had been a hay loft.

Mr Woollen spread his arms wide, palms uppermost in a gesture of helpless surrender, said with a gracious smile, "Now, please forgive me, I will have to make my excuses as I have some work to do. What with being delayed by today's unfortunate events, having to talk to the police and such, I am somewhat behind. Please, feel free to wander round if you wish, or perhaps another, longer, visit at a later date when I can also offer tea and cake?"

We shook hands, thanked him, and proffering a little bow, he left us, disappearing into the office.

While we waited for the men to catch up from lingering in the previous yard, Aunt Madge took a few more photographs. She always enjoyed herself with her camera, claiming that she saw things differently through a lens. Elsie and I had taken advantage of a quick rest on the bench and my aunt took a photo of us sitting together, arms linked, heads together, smiling at the camera.

"We ought to be heading home," Alf said as he joined us, peering through the office window at a clock on the wall. "It's a bit of a walk back and dusk will be setting in before we know it."

I popped my head round the open office door to say another thank you to Mr Woollen, but he wasn't there. The office was empty, but I could hear voices floating down from upstairs; not loud enough to eavesdrop on what was being said, but loud enough to know that the conversation was not a particularly friendly one.

Laurie called to me to catch up, and I left whoever was arguing to their own concerns. Whatever they were, they were most certainly not mine to worry about on this lovely summer's evening.

14

TWO SWANS A-SWIMMING

A short, pleasant, walk along the riverbank with the slow-running water still a glorious blue reflecting the last of the day. To the west the sky was starting to develop fingers of pink and gold, with the promise of a glorious sunset. This was the River Taw from which the valley, and immediate area, gets its name. The Taw is a mere trickle where it rises on the slopes of Dartmoor, but joined by the tributaries of the Mole, Yeo and Little Dart after running north through forty-five miles of rolling countryside, it becomes much wider by the time it's reached Barnstaple, Appledore and the Bristol Channel. Back in the sixteen and seventeen hundreds the Taw, near the coast, was a deep channel able to accommodate huge, tall ships sailing to and from Europe, the Caribbean and the British Colonies, but all that ceased when the river began to silt up. (Or so I had discovered when reading a library book about the history of Barnstaple.) There had been a fair amount of illicit smuggling using the river – and the concealing high-hedged lanes – to bring contraband inland quickly and easily. I mentioned this to Laurie as we walked along, and he answered that he'd not be surprised to hear that such smuggling continued to this day.

"Cigarettes, alcohol, drugs. Who's to say what can be brought in at the coast and transported upriver in small boats?" he said.

"But isn't there a coastguard?" I asked.

"Yes, but they can't be in all places all the time, and smugglers of today are just as canny as they were in the past. The only difference, I don't think they use pack ponies now. Lorries and vans are more practical."

Two swans were gracefully sailing along in the water, one with her wings arched over her back as if she were Gloriana with that huge white ruff that Elizabethan ladies wore.

"I must take a picture!" Aunt Madge exclaimed.

"Oh, look at the cygnets!" Elsie cried as a bevy of little birds plopped into the water behind their mum, who proudly bowed her slender neck and folded her wings.

"Cygnets really *do* hitch a lift on their mum's back!" Elsie added, delighted at our discovery.

The six babies were tiny little greyish balls of scruffy fluff, no long, elegant neck, no snow-white feathers, their little feet paddling like mad to keep up with the stately gliding of mum and dad. I immediately thought of *The Ugly Duckling* by Hans Christian Andersen. Laurie must have had the same thought because he burst into singing Danny Kaye's version of the tale about a cygnet who thought he was a duckling, making us all laugh with his expert rendition of the other birds picking on the poor little chap.

The effect was ruined by one of the little cygnets paddling towards us with what can only be described as an astonished expression of curiosity, no doubt thinking to himself what extraordinary oddities these human beings were. Daddy swan, the cob, had different ideas. We were threats. He rose out of the water, hissed loudly and flapped his great wings, water splashing everywhere, telling us most forcefully, to 'Clear off'.

We took the hint.

I suspect he gave his offspring a clip round the ear and told him or her not to fraternize with strangers.

"It isn't true that a swan can break someone's arm with their wings, you know." Alf said as we walked on, still giggling. Elsie, arm-in-arm with her husband, was continuing to hum the song to herself.

"It isn't," Uncle Toby said, "but I'd rather not get close enough to prove the point."

"It is true, however," Aunt Madge added, "that, technically, the Queen is the owner of all untagged mute swans swimming in open waters here in the U.K."

"How on earth do you know all these sorts of things?" Elsie asked.

"It's just one of those general knowledge things that I happen to know," Aunt Madge answered with a careless sort of shrug.

Uncle Toby chuckled. "And the fact that my wife knows that, as a young police constable, my very first arrest was for two men poaching swans with the intention of illegally selling them for meat."

"Ugh," I said, wrinkling my nose, "I wouldn't like to eat swan."

"Probably not much difference from goose," Uncle Toby suggested.

"Goose is delicious," Elise confirmed, "though it can be a bit fatty and greasy."

"Takes a brave person to confront an angry gander," Alf offered. "Or an angry swan, come to that!"

On the far bank a herd of black and white cattle

were grazing. Several raised their heads to solemnly stare at us. Two were lying down, chewing the cud.

"As they're not all lying down," I mused aloud, "does it mean a prediction of occasional showers, rather than heavy rain?" I never did truly understand the logic of that particular old wives' tale.

I walked hand in hand with Laurie, a perfect summer evening. We came to the footpath and turned up it. With the sun sinking and the day fading, the shadows were deep beneath the trees. Alf pointed out badger and deer tracks and I couldn't help wondering how the deer we'd freed from the fence was doing. The only things to spoil the walk were the midges that buzzed around. Elsie produced a fly repellent spray from her bag. It smelt pleasant but didn't do much to deter the annoying pests.

Bess was pleased to see us when we reached home. Alf fetched glasses and a bottle of champagne from the fridge, and we sat beneath the Go Outside gazebo, nibbling chunks of cheese and pineapple speared together on wooden cocktail sticks, and sipping our bubbly while watching as the stars, one by one, appeared, and the bats performed their incredible acrobatics. (Does the word come from bats, I wonder, or the other way round?)

"Despite everything that has happened," Elsie said with a broad, happy smile, "I've had a lovely day. Thank you everyone."

Alf topped our glasses up from a second bottle of fizz, and I was feeling quite tipsy by the time bedtime came around. It had been a long, eventful day, and although I had a lot to think about, I fell asleep almost immediately and slept like a log. Cuddling my teddy Bee Bear, of course.

15

BLACK BOOKS

The next morning, Monday, Ralph Greenslade was not very pleased. In fact, he was furious. So cross that he knocked at Valley View Farm's back door at just gone nine in the morning. (Unless they were strangers or formal visitors, most people living in the country use the back door, not the front.) We were all up and dressed, waiting patiently for the cooked breakfast that Aunt Madge and Elsie had on the go. Laurie answered the door and invited him in.

"We're about to have breakfast. Sit yourself down; there'll be enough for you as well," Elsie offered, indicating a chair at the large kitchen table by waving a baked-beany spoon at it.

"No thank you, Mrs Walker. But I wouldn't say no to a cup o' tea."

Alf duly fetched an additional cup and poured.

"Now then, what's wrong?" Laurie asked.

"It be them blitherin' coppers. Been tramplin' an' drivin' all over the meadow, flattenin' the hay, and now this mornin', I goes up to give it a last turn an' that idiot young ninny won't let me through the gate."

Uncle Toby frowned. "Whyever not? Surely, they don't need to keep the entire meadow sealed off as a crime scene? I can understand the patch where the body was found, perhaps, but it's clear the poor lad was killed in the woods, not the meadow.

"And the woods are *not* sealed off," Laurie said. "I took Bess for a walk there early this morning."

"What? Without me?" I complained, affronted at being left out.

"You, my lovely," Laurie said leaning forward to kiss my cheek, "when I peeped round the door, were sound asleep in bed, cuddling that teddy bear of yours and snoring soundly."

"I was not snoring!" I protested.

Laurie grinned. "You were snoring, and you were cuddling that bear. I was extremely jealous."

"You wait until winter," Aunt Madge chuckled. "She'll also have two hot water bottles and fluffy, pink bed socks."

"Aunt! That's my secret!" I protested again, but laughed.

Uncle Toby got to his feet. "Let me see if I can make a phone call, Mr Greenslade. I know Superintendent Moorcroft at Barnstaple, he might have an idea of what's going on."

We tucked into the breakfast set before us, ears wagging to listen to what my uncle was saying on the phone out in the hall. And despite his protestations, Elsie placed a plate of breakfast in front of Ralph Greenslade, who promptly tucked in with gusto.

Eavesdropping on a telephone call is very frustrating because you only hear one side of the conversation. We heard Uncle Toby asking to speak to the Superintendent, followed by, "Yes, I'm a friend. DCI Christopher... Yes... Thank you, I'll hold."

A long pause.

"Hello? Bernard?... Yes, I'm here in Devon for a long weekend... No, sorry I go back to London soon... Yes, next time. Look, I do not want to tread on toes but is it necessary to have the meadow where that unfortunate young man was found remaining sealed off? It has a rather valuable crop of hay waiting to be brought in... Yes, you've got a young PC on patrol at the gate, not letting the farmer or anyone in. Well yes, I assume that forensics have done all they need to do as well."

There was another long pause.

"DS Frobisher, I believe. Not my place to say, but the farmer would be most appreciative. Yes... Sorry? He hasn't? Oh, that's remiss. Gone away, you say? Perhaps because of the weekend? Yes, I'm happy to enquire if you think it wouldn't be interfering. What's that? Er, no I don't think we have any vacancies at present. Possibly, but London's not to everyone's taste. Yes, I'll keep it in mind. Thank you. And yes, we must meet for a drink next time I'm here. Goodbye."

Uncle Toby came back into the kitchen and sat down. Elsie placed a large plate of eggs, sausages, fried bread, bacon and baked beans in front of him.

"Moorcroft is going to speak with the DI in charge and send word that the constable can take any tape down and return to the station. Give it about an hour, Mr Greenslade, then the meadow will be all yours. It seems that not all statements have been gathered in yet. De Lainé is not in his caravan, apparently gone away or something. No one in the village has seen him since yesterday lunchtime."

The conversation turned to other matters while seconds were served to those of us who eagerly held up empty plates – Mr Greenslade included.

"So, what are our plans for today?" Laurie asked,

sitting back in his chair and resting his hands on what looked to be a rather full belly. I knew exactly how he felt.

"I'll give the hay one more turn," Mr Greenslade said. "Give 'er a chance to dry and fluff up agin."

Laurie bit back an amused laugh. "I thought that was merely a townsman's term," he joked. "I didn't think you farmers would use something as mundane as 'fluff up'."

Mr Greenslade maintained a solemn face. "What'd we be callin' 'er instead then? We fluffs it up because she be needin' fluffin' up." He guffawed. "Fluffin' up is what 'tis. Any road, come early af'noon I'll bale. I wouldn't be surprised if'n this wind turns, she'll bring in rain by this evenin'."

"If that's the case, we'll all help," Alf said. "Better to get it in and stacked rather than soaked and ruined."

"Aye, I'd be appreciatin' that Mr Walker." Mr Greenslade touched his forehead in a sort of salute to acknowledge thanks for his breakfast, then left, heading in the direction of hopefully restarting work with his tractor.

Elsie started clearing away empty dishes. "Someone needs to fetch the bread from the village shop. Milk and butter's been delivered already by the local dairy, but I'll need the bread, oh and some coffee. And we're almost out of digestive biscuits. And I could do with some more washing powder. Normally I'd be doing the laundry on a Monday, with cold meat, mash and pickle for dinner, but I can't be doing with getting the twin tub out today, not with guests and the hay to be brought in. Wash day can wait, no rush."

"I remember you having to get the old copper out, boiling hot water and doing the laundry by hand," Laurie said. "Rubbing the laundry on the washboard, and that old hand mangle; me feeding sheets and shirts through those rollers, while you turned the handle. Great big green, iron thing it was. What happened to it?"

Alf got up from the table to make a fresh pot of tea. "Rag and bone man took it when I bought your mum the Hotpoint Twin Tub. It's a wonder more people didn't get their fingers or hands squashed in those mangles."

Elsie laughed, "I remember one time I was doing the wringing and my apron got caught up in a roller. I panicked and kept rolling, until I realised I had to turn the handle in reverse. Maybe lamb chops from the butcher for dinner tonight, if that suits everyone?"

"Make a list," Laurie suggested. "I'll pop into South Molton."

"Is there a photographer's shop in town?" Aunt Madge asked. "I've three film rolls I need developing. If they can do them before we leave for home tomorrow morning, that would be useful."

"A good one," Alf said, "is Roger's. He's very efficient."

"No buying a new camera," Uncle Toby admonished, stirring sugar into his tea. "I know you when you get in those sorts of places."

Aunt Madge pretended to be peeved.

"The shops this morning, back here for lunch, then donning our smocks, clogs and straw hats for haymaking," Laurie said, planning the day's activities.

I hoped he was joking about the old-fashioned smocks and clogs.

"What was that last thing you said to Moorcroft about 'no vacancies'?" Aunt Madge asked.

Uncle Toby took a sip of tea. "Frobisher's got himself into the superintendent's black books for not getting on with things. He's wondering whether to suggest that Frobisher looks for a transfer."

Laurie groaned. "Not in our direction, I hope?"

Uncle Toby made no reply, which meant he agreed.

I sat very quiet. Black books? I'd remembered something.

16

WHAT IF...?

"Oliver de Lainé had a black book," I said, carefully thinking back in case I'd got muddled somehow. "Don't you remember, Laurie? He was looking for it when we were up at the shop on Friday. He said it was black with a racehorse embossed on it."

"Oh, yes. His address book. I thought he was rather showing off with his elaborate name dropping, mentioning Elizabeth Taylor and those top Hollywood stars. I wonder if he really does know any of them?"

From the sink where she was starting to do the washing up – firmly refusing any offers of assistance – Elsie interjected. "You're on a loser there, son. Mr de Lainé has been in several very big films alongside more than a few top actors and actresses. He was well known for minor parts before the war, then starred in many of those wartime propaganda films made by British Pathé. In the late '40s he was enticed to Hollywood. It's only these last few years that he's dropped out of the limelight."

"Why wasn't he called up, then?" Alf asked disdainfully. "He must be in his fifties now, twenties during the war. Parading about in front of a camera instead of fighting for his country? Shameful."

Elsie flicked soapy water at him. "He was in the RAF, dear. Was shot down and injured during the Battle of Britain. When he recovered, Pathé recruited him via the War Office, or Home Office, or whatever it was for their 'do your bit' films. He was popular because he was very handsome back then."

"Why haven't I heard much about him?" I asked.

"Have you seen *Day of the Golden Eagle* or *Dawn of the Tiger*?"

I shook my head. I knew his name and had heard of these films, but they weren't my sort of cinema enjoyment.

"He's played prominent parts in several Shakespeare productions, too."

"Ah, hence the *Romeo and Juliet* quotes?" Laurie said.

"None of that explains why he's here in Devon," Alf said sceptically and somewhat petulantly. I got the impression that my boyfriend's father didn't like Oliver de Lainé, while his wife was, maybe, somewhat enamoured by him?

"He was born in the West Country. Now, unfortunately, excessive drink, over-indulged gambling, and advancing age has caused his career downfall, so he spends time in his homeland where he can maintain his privacy," Elsie promptly and knowledgably answered. Yes, there was definitely a touch of disappointment about his apparent fall from grace in her voice. "He started coming to Chappletawton for the summer back in 1968. I remember because that's when Heather got her Postmistress status and took over running the shop, instead of being an assistant. He was a pinup of hers. Mine as well. Heather and I used to go off to the pictures in Barnstaple together, do you remember, Alfred? Leaving you to babysit Lawrence."

(I must add, here, that Elsie, as Laurie's mum, was the only one who called him Lawrence, not Laurie.)

Laurie protested. "I don't think I needed babysitting in 1967 Mum."

"No, no, silly, I meant when you were a young boy. *The Day of The Golden Eagle* came out in 1957; you were ten. Oh, it was such a romantic film! De Lainé was a Russian in love with a young married woman. She had to choose between him or her husband and son, but, out of remorse, ended the affair by hanging herself."

"As in *Anna Karenina* or *Dr Zhivago*?" I offered.

"Oh, don't get her started on Omar Sharif!" Alf rolled his eyes in mock horror. "He's another of her star-struck cinema loves."

"Didn't Anna Karenina kill herself by throwing herself under a train?" I asked.

"Yes, so tragic. Have you not read the book?" Alf queried.

"Tolstoy's rather *long*," I hesitated, not wanting to sound like a Philistine.

"What she means is, he's tedious and there's no starship battles or mad aliens dashing about – my Jan's into science fiction, not Cossack sagas." Laurie was right. I loved sci-fi and was determined to have the novel I was attempting to write published one day.

Uncle Toby chipped in, "Pasternak's *Zhivago* was smuggled out of Stalin's Russia and published by an Italian company. He went on to win the Nobel prize for literature, but was forced by the Communists not to accept it. A shame, it's actually a wonderful novel."

"Wonderful stories or not," Elsie interrupted, "Heather changed her mind about de Lainé when he started running up IOUs that he couldn't pay. And I decided I preferred Clint Eastwood and Tom Jones."

"Both of whom are absolutely *nothing* like my dad!" Laurie chuckled.

"I might not be as sexy as those two fellows, my boy, but *they* don't pay the bills round here, do they?"

Alf picked up a wooden spoon and using it as a pretend microphone started to sing *It's Not Unusual*, shimmying around the kitchen in Tom Jones fashion, before grabbing his wife and waltzing her around instead, changing the words to, "It's not unusual to be soap-sudded by anyone...!"

When we stopped laughing and, out of breath, Alf had sat down again, Aunt Madge, ignoring Elsie's protests, found a tea towel to start drying the washed dishes and asked, "Wasn't there a scandal about de Lainé? A rumour of a regrettable dalliance with the young wife of a top director, or something?"

"How on earth do you ladies know all these things?" Alf asked, quite astonished.

Elsie smiled serenely at him, then looked smug. "The *News of the World* my dear. The *News of the World*! And village gossip. You ought to come to the Thursday coffee mornings instead of working away in your strictly private office. You'd learn a lot."

Alf was an accountant and had a secluded room at the back of the house. He always kept the door locked because of client confidentiality, or so he maintained. Laurie had privately told me, during my previous visit at Christmas, that it was to hide the fact that he secretly read boys' comics, the *Beano* and *Dandy*. "He thinks we don't know, but of course we do."

"Er, the black book?" Uncle Toby interrupted, steering us back to the pertinent subject.

I explained. "I saw de Lainé arguing with O'Connor, on Friday afternoon when we went to the shop to buy tea. There was quite an altercation between them, ending up with the jockey storming off." I chewed my lip, then added doubtfully, "I can't be sure what the argument was about, something to do with O'Connor wanting something from de Lainé, which he didn't have. What if it was this black address book? De Lainé had lost it, he had come back into the shop looking for it. Perhaps he thought that O'Connor had it?"

"There was no black book in O'Connor's pockets when we found him," my uncle said.

"Doesn't mean he didn't have it," I replied. "He could have put it somewhere safe, or whoever murdered him took it. Perhaps, even, that was why he was murdered? Someone wanted that book?"

"Fair enough, sweetheart," Laurie answered, then added in his policeman's voice, "but why would a jockey want a film star's address book?"

"Blackmail for a black book?" I promptly suggested.

"Lots of people," Elsie declared, "would want to get their hands on such a book if it contains telephone numbers and addresses of famous people. Journalists especially. They would pay a fortune to get their hands on it, I expect. I'd wager even you, Lawrence dear, would not turn your nose up at Elizabeth Taylor's personal telephone number!"

Laurie had the good grace to blush slightly. Did he like her then? I hadn't realised.

I briefly wondered about wearing my eye makeup to resemble the elaborate style of her in the title role of *Cleopatra*, but then reasoned that I was nowhere near as beautiful as she was, so I'd be wasting my time and eyeliner. Alas.

17

PRETTY PICTURES

I liked shopping in South Molton, a picturesque country town comprising a blend of the old, mostly Georgian, buildings and the new 1970s modern. It was not market day, so the pannier market where crafts, flowers, fruit, veg, pies, pasties, cheeses and delicious smelling new-baked bread were sold was closed, but there were plenty of shops instead. Laurie went to fulfil his mum's shopping list while Aunt Madge and I entered Roger's Photographic Emporium, a few doors up from the pannier market entrance.

'Emporium' was a rather grand title, but maybe Aladdin's Cave would have been more appropriate, for displayed on the shelves was every type of camera imaginable along with accompanying equipment, and in between on the walls, dozens of photographs. Big ones, small ones, medium-sized ones. Black and white, colour, sepia; portraits, landscapes, still life – quirky, or mundane, and each one was magnificent! Aunt Madge is a watercolour artist (of some repute, I might add) and she was enchanted at not only the subject matter of the photographs, but the skill of capturing light against shade, the composition, the angle of the shot – the sheer entrancement of a perfectly balanced photograph.

"Are any of these for sale?" she asked, peering closer at a girl in shadow with the background of a sun kissed Dartmoor Tor rising majestically behind her.

"Ah, that's my daughter," the man behind the counter said, coming forward to inspect the photograph. "I took it, what, six years ago now. Must admit the way I captured the light I'm very pleased with it. No, sorry, not for sale. Just for show."

"And a very good show it is. Are these all yours?" Aunt Madge asked.

"They are. My gallery, as it were."

"You deserve a wider audience. You are Mr Rogers I assume?"

The man nodded. "Roger Rogers at your service ma'am. Ridiculous name, I have no idea what my unimaginative parents were thinking of."

I could sympathise there, having been Christened 'January'. (I'll add, he said ma'am as in 'jam', not as in 'farm', which must have edged him up another notch in my aunt's esteem.)

They chatted for a while about photography, and I was getting anxious that perhaps my aunt was leaning towards taking up the hobby, which was fine but would be expensive. I sighed with relief when she said, "I'm afraid I've not come to buy anything, merely to ask how long it would take to develop the three rolls of film that I have."

Roger Rogers looked disappointed, but quickly brightened. I guessed he didn't sell much high-priced costly stuff here in South Molton, but was always hopeful.

"As it happens, I'm twiddling my thumbs slightly today, we're not yet into the tourist season, you see. I could get them done by early tomorrow morning for you."

"That would be wonderful, thank you. I'm off back to London tomorrow. I could collect them before we leave, perhaps? My husband and I are staying with the parents of my niece's fiancé at Chappletawton."

At that moment, Laurie walked into the shop lugging a heavy shopping bag. "Hello Mr Rogers!" he said. "You look well. How's that lovely daughter of yours?"

OK, I was miffed. From the photographs I could see how lovely this daughter was. She could easily have been a film star as glamorous as Liz Taylor, but Mr Rogers said that she had been a groom at Mr Woollen's training yard. She was now at university. Several of the photos were of racehorses galloping against misty, ethereal background scenery, and a few were artistic portrayals of work around the stableyard. Several had her in them. How on earth did she manage to keep that beautiful appearance while mucking out stables? I always looked hot, sweaty and dishevelled whenever I did Aunt Madge's horses.

Mr Rogers was beaming with pride. "She's doing very nicely, Laurie. She's halfway through her medical degree up north, training to become a doctor."

"Good for her," Laurie approved. "I'll never forget when we were kids, she was always insisting on bandaging pretend broken limbs and putting arms into slings."

"Aye, she takes after her dear departed mother for a choice of career. Anyway, leave your films with me Mrs ... er Mrs? I'll need a name, and I assume Valley View Farm?"

"Mrs Christopher, and yes, Valley View. Do I pay you now?"

"Yes please. Best to get the tedious stuff out of the way, I always think."

Aunt Madge settled the bill while I took another look at Mr Rogers' photographs. They really were very good. Most of my snaps, when I bothered taking any, usually resulted in half of the main subject missing, the photo looking like a post or tree was growing out of someone's head, or with my thumb over the shutter leaving a fuzzed blob covering one corner.

Returning to the village in the car, Laurie explained that before Mrs Rogers died the family had lived in the village. "Jackie and I grew up together," he said, "though back then she always said she wanted to be a vet, even though her mum was our local GP."

I know that niggle of jealousy should not have whispered in my ear, but I was heartily glad that the very pretty Jackie was safely somewhere 'up north'. I hoped that maybe Mr Rogers had meant Aberdeen, or better still, John O'Groats, far, far away in Scotland, though to a Devonian, 'up north' could as easily mean Bristol or Bath. I had no idea where any medical schools were, so was none the wiser. And I was, maybe, too churlish to ask?

Our village was about a twenty-minute drive from town, the roads getting narrower and more countrified the nearer we got to Chappletawton. Uncle Toby called the last lane to Valley View a goat track – which it wasn't quite, but not far off. The surrounding countryside of fields and woods were always a delight to look at. As we approached the village itself, Laurie suddenly had to slam the brakes on, making Aunt Madge and me gasp and Laurie swear under his breath. A girl, wearing a blue pinafore dress had run out in front of us, waving her arms.

"Mary-Anne Culpin! Are you trying to get yourself

killed?" Laurie roared as he leant out of the open driver's window.

"Mr Walker! Please come; it's Mrs Clack – she's dead!"

18

SCAREDYCROWS AND FISTICUFFS

Dorothy Clack's thatched cottage, Meadow View, was the first one in the village, a few yards ahead of us. Laurie pulled the car into the gateway, leapt out and ran after Mary-Anne who was urging him to follow. He was still berating her for jumping in front of the car and offering dire warnings that if this was a prank... Aunt Madge and I followed them along the crazy paving path to the back of the house where there was a neat little garden, filled with colourful beds of flowers, and in one corner, a vegetable patch sprouting runner beans, cabbages, peas and carrots. The entire pretty picture spoiled by a pile of old rags dumped on the daisy-covered lawn.

"Did you go inside?" Laurie was asking Mary-Anne, as he took a handkerchief from his pocket and folded it over the kitchen doorlatch.

"No, mister. I only peeped through the kitchin winder."

Laurie pressed the latch down, opened the door and went in. From behind him, where we stood on the threshold, we could see Mrs Clack on the floor. Very much dead, with baler twine wound tight around her neck.

"I'll call the police," Aunt Madge said. Without hesitation she turned around and sprinted in the direction of the village telephone box.

"Take the girl away, Jan, this isn't the place for her," Laurie advised, nodding towards Mary-Anne who was clearly upset.

"I didn't do it, miss," she said to me through threatening tears. "I didn't kill her. But I didn't know what t' do, then I see'd your car comin'..."

"Of course you didn't kill her, sweetheart, and you did the right thing to stop us. Come on, let's sit on that bench by Mrs Clack's front door, shall we?" I put my hands on the girl's shoulders and steered her away, leaving Laurie to have a discreet preliminary look round the cottage.

To my surprise, Mary-Anne stooped to pick up the bundle of old rags, and I realised it was Mr Dill's scarecrow, floppy from not having any supporting poles.

"What's he doing here?" I asked, fairly gently, but with a slight reprimand in my voice.

"I were goin' t' put 'im on 'er lawn. Give 'er a laugh." Mary-Anne admitted, shamefaced and scuffing one shoe in the gravel of the path.

"Unfortunately, I don't think Mrs Clack found a moving-about scarecrow very funny. How about we put him back where he belongs in the field? No questions asked about where he's been, *hmm*?"

Mary-Anne sniffed aside her tears. "I didn't mean t' 'urt no one miss! I thought t'were funny. But 'tisn't is it?"

"No, Mary-Anne it isn't. Not one bit. And why, might I ask, are you not in school today?"

"Got nits in't I? Teacher, Miss Appleby, don't want

me back 'til they've been zapped with that stinky 'orrible stuff Mam's got." She scratched at her short curly hair and I backed away a pace. I thought it best to return to the topic in hand.

"Let's get this scarecrow settled in the field where he belongs, shall we?"

"I can do it m'self, miss. 'E's not 'eavy, 'e's only an ol' scaredycrow sack, filled wiv straw."

I wondered whether she would simply put him somewhere else equally as silly, but then I thought, wherever she left him it would get her – and her nits – away from me and Mrs Clack's cottage.

Mary-Anne heaved the bundle of old clothes and straw-filled sack over her shoulder, and the poor scarecrow flopped even more. Something fell out of his coat pocket. I stooped to pick it up.

"Mary-Anne," I asked tentatively, "where did you get this book from?"

"Dunno miss, t'idn't mine."

I raised an eyebrow.

"Found it, didn't I. In the phone box."

From the embossed racehorse on the cover, I strongly suspected that this was Mr de Lainé's missing address book.

"I allus go int' phone box if I sees summon come out. Growed-ups forget t' press button B."

I had to smile at that, I remembered doing the same in the hope that 'B' would yield some uncollected pennies. I didn't have the heart to tell Mary-Anne that many of these old-style phone boxes were now redundant. The Chappletawton box must be one of the few as yet unreplaced by newer versions.

"The man asked me if I'd stole it," Mary-Anne was saying. "That were a bloomin' cheek, that were! I tol' 'im no, but when I thort about it, I had *found* it after he'd used the 'phone. P'raps I should've said? But I didn't, I 'id it in the scaredycrow's pocket. You won't tell Mam will 'ee? Only the man gave me some sweeties, an' I ain't s'posed to take sweeties from men."

"What man was this, Mary-Anne?"

"That toffee-tod Mr D. Layne. What's the 'd' fer miss?"

"It's French, *de Lainé*."

She snorted. "'E don't sound like no Frenchie. Least, not like they speak on telly. You know," she held her nose, "*he-haw, he-haw, he-haw*."

De Lainé? I was starting to have an uneasy feeling about him.

"When was this, Mary-Anne? When did he speak to you?"

"Friday 'twere. After I see you an' Mr Walker goin' into the woods." She grinned, "Proper sweet'earts you be. All kissy kissy! He'd been in an' out the phone box sev'rl times that af'noon. Arguing like Father does when 'is tea bain't ready."

I wondered who he had been arguing with as I put the address book in my own pocket, and ignored the 'kissy kissy' bit. "No, I won't tell anyone about the sweeties. Now, off you go. Put that scarecrow back where he belongs, then go home and stay there because a policeman might want a word with you about finding Mrs Clack, but we won't mention the address book. It'll be our secret."

Mary-Anne paled. "Is 'e goin' t' lock me up fer bein' naughty?"

Ah, an opportunity to put an end to her idea of a joke. "As long as you promise not to play any more pranks on anyone, then no, the policeman will not lock you up."

She brightened at that, grasped the battered scarecrow tighter, but before she disappeared asked another question. "Why d'you call it an address book? T'ain't got no addresses, just lots o' numbers."

"Well, address books are sometimes used for telephone numbers."

She nodded at that, and trotted off up the lane, looking back once over her shoulder, remarked, "Funny lookin' 'phone numbers though, miss."

I frowned and decided to take a look at the contents of this famous – infamous? – book. I fiddled with the clasp that kept the pages closed, but it was small and stiff.

"I won't ask why a child is lugging a scarecrow around," Aunt Madge said, appearing at my side. "The police are on their way."

I tucked the book back into my pocket, and indicating the retreating Mary-Anne offered a brief explanation: "I think the village might stay quieter for a little while. No more scarecrows walking about. Did you press button 'B'?"

"Button B? Whatever for?" Then she twigged. "In my day we used to stuff a small rag up the chute, then come back later and remove it, hoping a lot of stuck coins would drop down."

"And did they?"

"Oh yes, quite often."

"Well, don't tell Mary-Anne, I don't think she's thought of that trick yet."

We went around to the back of the house. Laurie was waiting by the open door. He'd covered Mrs Clack with a blanket.

"I've had a quick look round; nothing seems out of place. Doesn't look like a burglary, her purse is in her handbag. She's quite cold, too, probably been lying there some while. Possibly since yesterday."

I peered in through the window, shielding my eyes with my hand to see clearer. "Two cups and saucers on the table and a plate with biscuit crumbs? Did she have a visitor?"

Laurie nodded. "Yes, well spotted. Two cups. The crumbs are stale, and the teapot and kettle are stone cold. Milk in the jug is on the turn, too."

"Is her husband home?"

"No sign of a husband living here," Laurie said. "No men's clothes in the wardrobe, no shaving stuff in the bathroom. If she still has a husband, I'd say he disappeared long ago."

"So, she had a visitor, but not a recent one?" Aunt Madge thoughtfully concluded.

"A visitor. But who?" I echoed. My hand went to my pocket. Oliver de Lainé? Still looking for his missing address book? Mary-Anne said he'd asked about it and offered her sweets. I'd seen him arguing with the jockey, even threatening him. Mrs Clack had been in the shop where he'd thought he'd lost the book, not realising that Mary-Anne had found it in the phone box. Had he been pestering Dotty Dorothy, perhaps? He'd not been very happy at the races on Saturday afternoon, then he'd suddenly disappeared from the pub Sunday lunchtime and hadn't been seen since. A voice behind me made me jump.

"What are you lot doing here nosing around? Not interfering with my case again, I trust?"

DS Frobisher was standing there, hands stuffed into his pockets, face with an expression that would have solidified melted lard.

"You got here quick," Laurie said. "Mrs Christopher only telephoned five minutes ago."

"What do you mean? I'm here to bring the old bird in for questioning. We have reason to believe she's answerable for the murder of Ruairi O'Connor. She claims she found a body, which you, Walker, went to investigate instead of calling the local police. You found nothing, because she had already moved the corpse. Under caution she is to help with our enquiries."

Laurie moved aside from the kitchen door and gestured with his hand for Frobisher to enter. "Good luck with that then. She's dead."

For a moment the detective sergeants stared at each other like dogs squaring up for a fight. Frobisher backed down first, and 'hrrumphing', went into the house, yanked back the blanket and stared down at the dead woman.

"Who found her?"

"A child. Mary-Anne Culpin from the village. We sent her home, being near the deceased is not for kiddies."

"Huh, you'd be surprised. The horrid little beasts are as tough as old boots round here. You touch anything?"

"I had a quick look round, but no, didn't touch anything, apart from the blanket that was on the settee in the living room. No sign of forced entry. Doesn't look as if it was theft motivated."

"I'll be the judge of that, Walker," Frobisher snapped.

We heard a siren wailing. The cavalry from South Molton, responding to Aunt Madge's telephone call.

"I'll thank the three of you to vacate the premises, else I might start wondering what you're doing here."

"We were about to leave," Laurie said, ushering us away from the kitchen door with a shooshing motion of his hands.

"I hope you've not poked your nose any further into my case," Frobisher accused from behind us as we walked to the front of the cottage. "Else I might have to take you in for perverting the course of enquiry."

You're the pervert, I thought.

A crowd had gathered in the lane – in these valleys

the sound of sirens carried quite a way, and Mary-Anne, instead of going home, had dumped the scarecrow in his field and had been quick off the mark to divert any suspicious attention from herself by informing villagers that Mrs Clack, "Were as dead as a doornail!"

Unfortunately, she also added, loudly, "I told Mr DS Walker, as he be clever. He'll find the murderer an' lock 'im up, don't fret abou' that'!"

Frobisher was furious. His fists clenched as he glared from Laurie to Mary-Anne and back to Laurie, then began poking him in the chest.

"You come down here, Walker, playing the high and mighty know it all, sun shining from your holier than thou backside, poncing about with your bit of posh totty, who, frankly, looks like she could do with someone experienced to give her a good..."

Laurie hit him.

19

INTERLUDE - LAURIE

It's amazing how far blood can spurt from a single punch to the nose. Even if it (fortunately? Unfortunately?) isn't broken. I was spattered by the fountain that erupted from Frobisher's proboscis, enough of it also decorating the white wall of Mrs Clack's cottage. Forensics would have a field day.

Assaulting a police officer is not a good idea. Even if a quick, reckless jab with a clenched fist is entirely justifiable. Especially if the assault is made by another police officer, and even if the gathered crowd heartily applauded and cheered – a crowd which included my boss's wife and my future wife.

Frobisher did not see the entertaining side of it, but sat on the bench by the cottage's front door mopping blood with a rapidly reddening handkerchief.

"Cor," I heard young Mary-Anne exclaim from within the crowd, "this is a lot more fun than playin' wiv scaredycrows."

"I'll have your warrant card for this Walker," Frobisher sniffed, dabbing at his nose. "I'll have you demoted to uniform. You'll be doing Traffic for the rest of your damned career."

Mrs Christopher waded in before I had a chance to answer. "And you, Detective Sergeant, will be filing a full report of exactly how you have grossly offended my niece by making lewd, suggestive insinuations about her in public. But before that, perhaps you would care to explain exactly what you meant, to her uncle and guardian, Detective Chief Inspector Christopher? I am sure he would be most interested to hear your excuses."

Mrs Christopher didn't wait for an answer but turned away from Frobisher and addressed Jan who was standing wide-eyed with her hands over her mouth. I must admit, I'm not sure if she was covering up her horror that I'd hit the utter piece of rubbish, or was laughing about it.

I'd thought it a few times before, but it entered my mind again: Mrs Christopher would be indomitable as someone in a position of authority, a High Court judge, or even Prime Minister, if it was ever likely that a woman could have that position. Personally, I can see absolutely no reason why not. Women are wonderful at organising and management. Why not organise and manage that sour lot in Parliament? Maybe a strong woman would keep them sober and awake a bit more often.

Mrs Christopher asked Jan to telephone Valley View and ask her uncle to come up to the village, but Frobisher held up his hand, stopping her from scooting off up the lane to the telephone box. DCI Christopher, despite not being connected to the police force down here was almost as formidable as his wife, and a personal friend of the local Chief Superintendent. One word from him and Frobisher could be out on his ear – as easily as I could be for drubbing a fellow officer, no matter how much he deserved it. We both of us knew the consequences of our actions.

"I apologise," Frobisher snuffled, removing the handkerchief to display a discoloured nose that was already swelling to twice its normal size. "But I'll not have you, Walker, trudging your size nines all over my case!"

That was fair enough, except I hadn't trudged anywhere near it.

"Your case, is your case," I retorted. "Beyond an initial foray into the woods and my giving a clear and concise statement, this murder – or the previous one – has nothing to do with me."

"Yet you undermine my cordoning off a murder scene. You interfere with a possible suspect this morning..."

"Now hang on!" I protested. "That field needs to have its hay baled, you do not need to cordon it off, and I was not – am not – interfering with your case. Mrs Clack is – was – not a suspect."

"So why *are* you here, eh? Tell me that DS Walker, and make it good."

"We were passing; the distressed child stopped us. Even you would not expect me to simply ignore her and drive on. Or would you?"

"I'll be checking that claim. It had better be the truth."

I bunched my fists. "Are you calling me a liar, DS Frobisher?" How I didn't hit him again, I'll never know.

"For goodness' sake!" Mrs Christopher bellowed. "Can you two hear yourselves? You are like two jealous schoolboys squabbling over an illicit cigarette behind the bicycle sheds!"

We both stared at her. I think my mouth was open, and then I burst into laughter. Mrs Christopher had got it in one. I'd never said anything before, but Frobisher and I had been squabbling like this since we were nine years old and in the same class at school. This wasn't the first punch on the nose I'd given him – and he'd given me many a black eye in return. He had always been a lazy, good-for-nothing who could never be bothered to put any exertion into anything. The times he had tried to copy my work at school, to bribe me to do his homework – to get me into trouble because he had (or hadn't) done something. Our rivalry had multiplied when the girl he'd fancied had preferred to go to a youth club dance with me, not with him. The girl in question had been Mr Rogers' daughter, Jackie. She'd chosen me because I was the better looking and far nicer guy. Although it might also have been because, when we were young kids, I had always been amenable to playing 'Casualty' with her... in the purely bandaging for first aid sense.

I later discovered, when Jackie had let something slip on one of our youth club dates, that Frobisher had pestered her to 'play doctor' in that other, unsavoury, sense. I'd given him a black eye for that. And yes, we had also squabbled about smoking illicit cigarettes behind the school bicycle sheds. I'd provided them, he'd smoked them. I admit it. I wasn't a very bright kid when it came to selecting school mates to hang out with.

"Yeah, well, he should stop pretending to be better than me," Frobisher grumbled.

How I longed to retort that I *was* better than him. Always had been. But I caught Mrs Christopher's hard stare and swallowed my pride. Paddington Bear's famous fictional Hard Stare is not a patch on Mrs. C's version. It wasn't worth contradicting.

"I apologise," I muttered, proffering my hand and half meaning it. "I should not have thumped you, and I have not intentionally had anything to do with your case." I took a deeper breath, reached my hand nearer to him. "No hard feelings? Quits?"

He grunted but reluctantly shook my hand. The crowd cheered and began to disperse, the show over.

I wanted to ask on what grounds he had decided to arrest Mrs Clack, but maybe he'd had good reason? There was every possibility that she had been lying through her teeth about finding a body. O'Connor was drunk, that was plain. Had she found him slumped, comatose in the clearing, taken an objection to his state and strangled him? Admitted, it didn't seem likely, but not impossible. Nor would it have been hard for her to move and hide the body. Difficult, maybe a struggle, but again, not impossible.

Except, now that she was dead the probability of her murdering the jockey seemed unlikely. What motive would she have had? And even more pertinent, what motive could there be for strangling her in the same way? There was, as I saw it, only one: whoever killed O'Connor believed that Mrs Dorothy Clack had either seen or heard something in the woods that she should not have seen or heard.

Chappletawton was a quiet Devonshire village where the crime level was usually restricted to minor incidents like a tractor swinging too close to the telephone box resulting in broken glass, which conveniently went unnoticed; or various acts of sabotage to a rival's vegetables entered for the annual village summer show. But not wishing to sound callous, I was on holiday. I had enough crimes of my own to solve when I returned to London, and, as DS Frobisher had explicitly made clear, two murders within days of each other were not mine to speculate upon.

I was fine with that, and as long as he kept his grubby paws away from my Jan, he could do what he liked, when he liked.

20

MAKE HAY WHILE THE SUN SHINES

Poor Laurie, he disliked DS Frobisher, and clearly thought he was incompetent at his job, but the case was *his* job, not Laurie's, so we had to walk away from it. I took my jacket off when we got back into the car, and I'm ashamed to say, I then completely forgot about the black book in the pocket. In my defence (feeble, I know), I was distracted by telling Aunt Madge and Laurie about Mary-Anne's antics with her 'scaredycrow' – yes, entirely feeble because that part of the story went with the other, but the first part took longer to recite than the short journey home. Then we met Ralph Greenslade and his tractor in the lane, and Laurie had to concentrate on reversing for about eighty yards uphill to allow the farmer to get to the gate into the hay meadow. Believe me, reversing uphill in a narrow high-hedged lane is not easy, although Laurie, being an experienced and police trained driver, made the manoeuvre seem simple.

We stopped to sort out when Mr Greenslade would be baling. (After lunch, he said.) The police had gone from the meadow – one thing less to worry about – except low on the horizon grey clouds were gathering, and the air had turned distinctly humid. Mr Greenslade said he thought there was a storm coming, and wanted to press on with one final turn before baling to ensure the hay was as dry as it could be.

Elsie had our lunch ready, another distraction, so all in all, the address book in my jacket pocket was completely forgotten about.

Bess barked during lunch, but it was only the postman leaving letters in the box by the gate. Alf finished the last of his pork pie and went to fetch them, coming back to inform that he could hear a tractor up in the meadow, so it was time to go a-haymaking. We'd already donned old clothes – sleeved shirts and jeans as hay can be very scratchy, so bare arms or legs, even on a hot day, wasn't a good idea. Not to mention the ticks that can transfer from long grass and bracken to bite and suck for blood on people and animals.

We walked up the hill, leaving Elsie at home as she had back problems, so heaving hay about was not an option for her. As we walked, Laurie remarked that it was very quiet. Was Alf certain he'd heard the tractor?

The reason for the silence became clear when we got to the gate. The tractor was immobile halfway down the field with a neat line of rectangular hay bales spread behind like the line of a ship's wake. Mr Greenslade and his eldest son, Kevin, were bent over the attached baler, with only their backsides visible.

Alf laughed. "Must be a record; the baler's broken down after only one row. We usually get to at least the second."

"What's up?" Laurie called as we reached the tractor. Mr Greenslade muttered a few mild expletives about something not working – I had no idea what he actually said – and Kevin added a few mumblings with his head inside the baler's mechanical workings. A couple more grunts and oaths and up popped his grinning face. "All fixed!"

"Do we take bets on how far we get before we have to stop again?" Laurie laughed.

"It be talk like that what jinx everythin'!" Kevin chuckled as his father climbed into the cab and switched the engine on. A moment later, the tractor was trundling off down the row, the baler scooping up the cut hay, packing it into slabs, automatically tying them together with two lengths of baler string and shooting the trussed rectangular bale out behind, before repeating the whole process. Mr Greenslade drove the tractor round the field in ever decreasing circles – or more correctly, odd-shaped squares. Down one row, along the bottom of the meadow, up the furthest row, across the top of the meadow, down the next row, along the bottom... coming at each turn closer to the middle of the field until there were only two rows left.

The only part of the meadow that he avoided was the small area down in one corner where the body had been discovered. The police hadn't said or advised anything, but consensus between us had been that, maybe, it was disrespectful to use that particular portion of hay. It would only have made one bale anyway, no huge loss, overall.

Our job, I discovered, was to follow the tractor and stack the bound bales in groups of six or eight in order to make the next step of loading them onto the trailer easier.

"Roll them," Kevin advised when he saw me lifting a bale by the string. "Less likely for the twine t' break an' easier on your back. Roll with the lie of the land, downhill."

It took a while to cover the entire field, walking up and down the rows – down was fine, up... the hill seemed to get steeper with each row. Funny how it didn't look steep from the top, but imitated Mount Everest from the bottom. (Slight exaggeration, but you know what I mean!) At last the tractor came to a stop, with (and we all cheered) no more breakdowns. Scattered across the field as if they were some form of crude artistic sculptures, were stacks of hay, baking in the heat of the haze-shimmering, airless afternoon. We were all somewhat sweaty and grimy, with sore backs and smarting hands, despite wearing gloves. But the work was only half done. Five-hundred bales of hay had to be transferred into the security of the barn before those blackening clouds came any nearer.

Mr Greenslade unhitched the baler and disappeared down the hill to Lower Valley View with the tractor in order to fetch up the large trailer. Elsie appeared with a basket containing flasks of tea and a cake tin which, when opened, revealed thick slabs of fruit cake and upside-down apple cake. We sat on some bales, greedily scoffing the lot, while surreptitiously eyeing those clouds gathering deeper behind the hills, looking every inch like some sort of mustering army or bank of invading aliens.

If I thought anything we'd done so far was backbreaking, hard work, I soon discovered that I'd been wrong. Stacking the bales on the trailer was *much* harder, even though I had one of the easier assignments. Aunt Madge and I were on the flat bed of the trailer receiving the bales that the men tossed up. We had to stack them one layer at a time, with each layer criss-crossing, otherwise, if they'd been simply one atop the other the whole lot would fall down. The first three layers were quite simple, but as the stack got higher, the bales had to be tossed higher, and we had to climb higher to keep up with the enthusiastic (and apparently untiring) bale-tossing men. I say it was hard work (it was!) but it was also a laugh. Teasing and banter between us, laughing as the tractor pulling the trailer lurched across the field from each six or eight stacked pile of haybales to the next. I had never felt as stiff and tired before, nor had I ever felt as wonderfully alive and happy.

Aunt Madge jumped down as the fourth layer began to grow, aware that she wasn't too confident at balancing on a lurching and swaying height, which left me to do the last two layers on my own, but I'd got into the swing of it by then, so didn't mind.

I suppose the trailer took about seventy bales. (I can't tell you exactly; I'm guessing as I lost count somewhere along the third layer.) Then the next fun bit... there was no way I could get safely down – balancing atop a trailer stacked high with bales of hay is a challenge, believe me. Outside of learning how to fly, or leaping into Laurie's outstretched arms in the hope that he'd catch me (both not an option), there was only one thing for it. I made myself a hollow in the centre of the top layer to ride the trailer all the way down the lane.

"Duck your head under the low trees!" Laurie called as Mr Greenslade set off negotiating the gate and the fairly tight turn from the meadow into the lane.

I have to say, it was one of the most thrilling things I'd ever done – and this included those scary, whizzy rides at the fun fair! The trailer was slow, very bumpy and rattly, and I could hear the occasional grinding of complaining brakes holding back the tremendous weight as we went down the steep hill, but the view above the hedges to across the fields was magnificent, and the ride itself was, well I can only describe it as exciting.

The unloading and stacking in the barn was quickly done by the menfolk who had followed on foot, then more hilarious laughter as we all piled on to stand on the emptied trailer as Mr Greenslade drove back up the hill, with us clinging on like mad to the metal rails. If ever there was a time to feel seasick, this was it! Talk about shake, rattle and roll!

Then the whole process started over again, for I think it was seven or eight trips. Each foray up and down the lane was accompanied by increasing heat and humidity. Behind the rounded, green Devonshire hills the previously blue sky was becoming darker and heavier. With the last load almost finished, we heard the ominous rumble of distant thunder, and as I rode the trailer down the hill for the final time – taking a peek at the now empty field, I caught the purple-pink flash of distant lightning.

It started to rain just as the last five bales were stacked in the barn.

21

IT NEVER RAINS BUT IT POURS

The storm came in with a vengeance, almost as if the wrath of God was making a point that two murders had been committed and no one was any further forward with finding the culprit. The rain was worse than the thunder and lightning, for it fell down in a sheer curtain, drumming against the farmhouse windows and beating a tattoo on the slate roof.

"There'll be flooding down in the valley," Alf remarked as he stood at the window looking out into the grey gloom that was obliterating most of the view. Thunder was rolling and grumbling, its angry claps echoing up and down the valley, making it difficult to work out where one growl started and the other ended. A ghoulish pinky-purple lightning was providing the almost constant pyrotechnic display.

There came a particularly bright flash, followed almost instantly by a loud craa..aaa..ck that shook the foundations of the house. I stifled an alarmed squeak and clamped my hands over my ears. I really didn't like thunder.

"Hello!" Uncle Toby cried, "something's been hit!"

Almost at the same time, the electric lights flickered, then went out.

"Power cut. A pole or wire's been struck somewhere," Elsie calmly announced, getting up from the sofa and making her way at a trot to the kitchen. She came back with two lit hurricane lamps. It wasn't yet dusk, but it could have been, the storm was so heavy.

"I'll light a few candles as well," Elsie said, "in case this cut lasts. You'd better stoke the Aga, Alfred, we'll want another pot of tea soon." The Aga was a wood burner, so it didn't matter that there was no electric power. Elsie seemed cheerful and relaxed, but then, as Laurie had reassured me, they were quite used to power cuts whenever a storm blew in.

"Not that we have many," Alf explained. "They usually tend to bother Exmoor or Dartmoor, or South Devon. We're fairly sheltered up here in this neck of the woods, but when one does come in, we know all about it."

"Thank goodness we got all the hay in," Laurie said from where he was sitting tinkering at the upright piano. He was a good player and often gave impromptu renditions of familiar tunes and songs.

"Aye, Ralph will be pleased that that's done and dusted, but there are quite a few fields of barley and wheat out there which might get a bit battered."

Another crash of thunder roared along the valley, so loud that we didn't hear the front door knocker at first – Bess did, though. She jumped up, barking.

"Now who the heck...?" Laurie said as he got up and went into the hall to answer it.

We heard voices, then a laugh, followed by Laurie urging someone to come in.

"You're soaked through, man! Come in; I'll get Dad to light the fire to dry you off." Laurie and another man came into the sitting room. I instantly recognised Mr Rogers, the photographer.

"Nay, I'm fine," he was saying, "it's just my socks and trouser bottoms... I preserved your carpet, my dear Mrs Walker, by taking my sodden shoes off at the door. It's gushing a fair imitation of a river out there down the lane, and a telephone pole has been hit up in the village. I expect a few households will be inconvenienced for a while."

"Where are you parked?" Alf asked, indicating that Mr Rogers should sit himself down. Elsie had disappeared to the kitchen to make a pot of tea and find some more cake.

"I pulled in by your barn doors, I hope that is suitable? I didn't want to block the lane, although I don't think anyone will be up or down with this going on outside."

Elsie came in with a tray laden with cups, saucers and a plate piled with slices of fruit cake.

"Goodness me, I didn't expect to be treated to such hospitality," Mr Rogers declared. "I thought I'd take a route via the village to get home in order to bring these, Mrs Christopher – your photographs."

He reached into his jacket pocket and brought out three folders of developed photographs, which he handed to an excited and thrilled Aunt Madge.

"I wasn't busy in the shop this afternoon, so I managed to get these done for you. Thought I'd drop them off, but hadn't bargained on this sudden Noah type downpour." He added, "You've a good eye for a good photograph. Some of those are most impressive."

Aunt Madge beamed as she started looking through, then passing her 'snaps' around for us all to see. A couple from the horse racing were a little blurred where she hadn't set the shutter speed correctly – or whatever it is you have to do to get a clear picture. The ones she took at Four Horseshoes stables were superb. The way she'd caught the foals was magnificent. The only one I didn't like was the photo of Elsie and me. Lovely of Elsie, with her warm smile. Me? I had my eyes closed, which spoiled the whole thing.

I was about to hand the photograph back to Aunt Madge when I spotted something. I looked again, screwing my eyes up and peering closer to see better. Was it? Yes, I was certain.

"Did DS Frobisher say they hadn't got a statement from Oliver de Lainé yet?" I asked.

Laurie nodded. "Yes, apparently he's disappeared."

"No he hasn't," I said, flourishing the photo. "He's in the flat above the office at Four Horseshoes... look, he's peering out of the window!"

22

FUNNY SORT OF TELEPHONE
NUMBERS

And that, of course, reminded me of the black address book which was still in my jacket pocket.

Elsie refused to think of Mr Rogers leaving while the rain still poured down by the bucketload – although the noisy part of the storm, the crash, bang, wallop, was now rolling away into the distance, thank goodness, so, between us, we filled Mr Rogers in with the ghastly goings on that had been happening in and around the village, while Laurie and Uncle Toby looked through Mr de Lainé's 'address' book.

"There are no names or addresses in here," Laurie eventually said. "Only what appear to be initials. This most certainly is not a Hollywood star's confidential contact information. A pity," he joked, "I'd have liked to have had a chat with the gorgeous Liz." He saw me scowl, went back to the original subject. "It's mostly numbers of some sort. I've no idea what they mean."

Alf was looking over Laurie's shoulder, then guffawed.

"I know what they are!" he declared. "They're betting odds. Look," he pointed out one or two, explaining as Laurie slowly turned the pages. "This column has the odds, 4-1, 5-1, 10-1... whatever. This column is the amount of the bet placed – only it's confusing because he only has the numbers, no £ signs next to them. And this column shows the amount won or lost."

He took the book from Laurie and peering closer at each page, sat down in one of the armchairs, his brow furrowed, and muttering to himself. Alf Walker was an accountant and enjoyed the occasional modest flutter on the horses; he understood numbers and betting.

After a moment he slapped the book with his hand. "Looks like he was running a right racket. Look, these initials. A couple are fairly straightforward if you allow for an outright guess: JW – Jack Woollen? RC – Ruairi O'Connor? MW. No idea who that is, no one springs to mind." He flicked to the beginning of the book. "These are dates I think, they go back a good couple of years, summer only. 6.69 is June, 7.69 July, 8.69 August. Then the same for 1970 and '71. Then more initials. NA. EX. CH. I'd hazard that's Newton Abbot, Exeter and Cheltenham race meetings. Back to '69, and there are quite a few winners – look, these figures tally with good odds." We were all gathered round now, looking as best we could over his shoulders.

Uncle Toby scratched at his ear, always a sign that he was thinking hard. "What do you reckon? Placing bets on fixed races?"

"Not all that easy to do, Toby," offered Aunt Madge. "Getting a guaranteed winner is nigh on impossible, especially in jump racing. Perhaps easier on the flat where horses are less likely to fall, but still no certainty."

"Knowing a horse that *won't* win can be less risky and more profitable than knowing one that will," Mr Rogers suggested. He had a good point.

"*I want what's owed me, or I'm...!*" I blurted out.

"That's what O'Connor shouted at de Lainé when they were arguing up in the village on Friday afternoon. I didn't hear the rest, but perhaps it was something like, 'or I'm not fixing any more races'?"

"But he didn't win," Elsie said. "He fell off in more than one race. Oh. Oh, I see – it's easier to fix who *won't* win."

"Precisely," Uncle Toby confirmed, with a small nod of his head. "He deliberately fell off."

"But Jack Woollen and de Lainé were not at all happy," Laurie said. "If the races were fixed – and I still don't see how falling off or not winning helped – why the glum expressions?"

"Good actors, maybe? Not wanting to draw attention by showing pleasure at losing a race?"

"Whatever else he may be, Oliver de Lainé *is* a good actor," Elsie stated assertively.

"Or O'Connor messed up. Maybe he wasn't supposed to fall off?"

"A good strategy," Alf proposed as a theory, "is to ignore the favourite and place bets on the other runners, then, where possible, ensure the favourite doesn't win. Result? A guaranteed pay out with no one any the wiser."

"Except for the racecourse bookies," Uncle Toby queried. "Wouldn't they soon spot the fraud?"

"It isn't fraud to back more than one horse, and the bookies will still be making money on the runners that didn't win," Alf countered. "They may start to be a bit suspicious, but as long as they're not losing out, they shouldn't be particularly bothered. It's the punters, the other people placing bets, who are cheated. Any deliberate fixing is fraud."

I think we all agreed there was something fishy going on, even if we weren't exactly sure what it was and we were, maybe, barking up the wrong tree.

"If memory serves me correct, the records in this book," Alf said slowly, leafing through the pages again, "only refer to these last few years, the recent summers when Oliver de Lainé's holiday visits to Chappletawton occur. Coincidence? Or by design? I'm assuming he knows our Mr Jack Woollen?"

"You do realise," Mr Rogers interrupted, "who Oliver de Lainé really is, don't you?"

We all stared at him, blank-faced.

Mr Roger Rogers' face broadened into a grin. "I've lived in this area all my life, my mum and dad before me. As it happens, my gran used to be a housekeeper at Four Horseshoes between the wars. Because of that, Mum knew the family well. I used to play with most of the cousins whenever they came to visit. We camped in the woods, swam in the river – rode the horses. It was a big place then, prosperous, a successful training yard, not going downhill as it is now."

We protested at that. Mr Rogers shook his head.

"Look between the cracks. Mr Woollen rarely has good wins. Yes, here and there in insignificant races, but nothing big. He employs – sorry, employed – a third-rate jockey, staff come and go as often as the wind changes. The youngstock he sells he practically gives away because no one wants horses with poor pedigrees. Well known owners ceased sending him their horses yonks ago. It's a wonder he still has the money to keep going."

"Or perhaps he hasn't," Laurie said slowly, thinking aloud. "Which is why he's into fixing races."

"But what has Mr de Lainé to do with any of this?" I asked.

Aunt Madge made a plausible suggestion. "Jockeys and trainers can't bet. Mr de Lainé can. He puts the money on for the three of them."

Mr Rogers chuckled. "And you are all missing

something extremely relevant. None of you speak French, I assume?"

Aunt Madge bridled a little. "I do. Fluently."

Mr Rogers raised one eyebrow, questioningly.

"Oh," she said slowly, light dawning. "Oh, I think I see."

Mr Rogers nodded. "*Oui, madame, très bien.* Lainé changed his rather dull British name to something more glamorous when he began his acting career – much like Archibald Leach became Cary Grant, or Arthur Stanley Jefferson became Stan Laurel. *Lainé* is French for 'woollen'. Oliver de Lainé's real name is Michael Oliver Woollen. Jack Woollen's cousin."

23

HORSES FOR COURSES

Fortunately, the telephone pole that had been lightning blasted did not affect our telephone line. Laurie had felt obliged to telephone DS Frobisher, who considered himself not obliged to turn out of an evening in the pouring rain to listen to what he clearly thought was an interfering, crackpot hypothesis. He was interested in the fact that Oliver de Lainé had been at Four Horseshoes though, and was very possibly still there. Which, as it turned out, and as we discovered the next day, he was.

The storm had quite gone, and it was a lovely morning. Blue sky, shining sun, not too hot, with everything washed clean and fresh. That delicious aroma of damp earth mingling with whiffs of cut hay and summer vegetation filled the air. The electrics had come on again at about eleven that evening, not that I noticed for I'd sought my bed by ten o'clock, utterly shattered from the afternoon's work in the hay meadow.

Aunt Madge and Uncle Toby had set off for home straight after breakfast, driven by Alf in his car to Umberleigh, where they were to catch the train to

Exeter St David's, then the main line to London. I was sad to see them go (and I'm certain that Aunt Madge had a tear in her eye, as she loved it in Devon), but unlike Laurie, who had the rest of the week off, Uncle Toby had to get back to work. Someone competent had to keep watch on the London suburb criminals. Elsie went with them, intending to do some shopping in South Molton, which meant that Laurie and I had the house to ourselves.

We were enjoying freshly percolated coffee, taking advantage of the glorious sunshine filtering into the gazebo when Bess started barking. Laurie went round the side of the house to see what the fuss was about and reappeared a moment later with DS Frobisher in tow.

"I met your dad's car further up the lane," the policeman grumbled as, uninvited, he sat down. "I had to reverse. Going somewhere are they?"

"Why do you ask? Are we being warned not to leave town or something?" The hostility in Laurie's voice was plain. I got up to fetch another cup. We couldn't very well not offer coffee as the percolator was there, gently steaming, on the table.

"Leave it out, mate," Frobisher drawled. "We're supposed to be on the same side, aren't we? Catching the criminals, not barking at each other?"

I guessed from Laurie's tight-lipped silence that several sarcastic retorts were swimming through his mind. I turned to look at him, my frown indicating that he was not to even consider punching the man again. Satisfied that Laurie was going to keep his fists to himself I fetched the cup, and poured Frobisher a coffee, deliberately stirred in one sugar, not the two he'd asked for.

"We're bringing Oliver de Lainé in at this moment," Frobisher said. "Suspected of murdering the jockey

Ruairi O'Connor. He should be on his way to Barnstaple as we speak. We'll be grilling him as soon as I get there. If you've information I should know about, as you indicated on that very crackly telephone line last night, I would appreciate hearing it."

I went back indoors to fetch the black book; solemnly handed it to him.

"Where did this come from?" Frobisher asked suspiciously.

"It belongs to Oliver de Lainé," I explained. "He'd lost it and has been frantically looking for it. One of the village children found it and gave it to me to pass to him. It was only last night, being stuck indoors because of the storm, that we realised its significance," I partially lied. I had no intention of telling him the full information.

Laurie let him stare, uncomprehending, at its contents for a few minutes, before putting the man out of his puzzled ignorance.

"We think these are to do with some sort of betting fraud." He patiently outlined our conclusions from the night before, including giving de Lainé's real name, which Frobisher clearly had no knowledge of.

Frobisher glanced through the book again. "So, this is something thought up by the three of them? Woollen as trainer, de Lainé as the bet placer and the jockey nobbling the races?"

"That's what it looks like," Laurie agreed.

"Motive for murder?"

"O'Connor wanted out, perhaps? Maybe they weren't paying him enough. He was taking all the risks, after all."

Frobisher sipped his coffee, grimaced and helped himself to more sugar. "Explain Dorothy Clack. What had she to do with all this? Who did her in, and why?"

Laurie shrugged. "Could have been either de Lainé

135

or Jack Woollen. I'd hazard that whichever one of them strangled O'Connor, also killed Mrs Clack. Motive? He thought Mrs Clack was a witness. He hadn't realised that she was also in the woods. When he discovered that she'd found the body, her fate was sealed. That was partly our fault, unfortunately. We were in the Exeter Inn. De Lainé was there, overheard everything. Woollen came in searching for his missing jockey, caught us talking about Mrs Clack and her whimsical fantasies – in this instance, a dead leprechaun in the woods."

Frobisher stared at us, none the wiser. "Leprechaun?"

"Mrs Clack had met him before and knew that he was Irish, so, in her imaginative fantasy world, concluded that he was one of the wee folk. A leprechaun," I said.

Frowning, Frobisher was working things out, slowly, in his head. "But if Woollen was actively looking for O'Connor, that makes the suspicion fall firmly on de Lainé's shoulders."

"Not if Jack Woollen was pulling the wool over our eyes, covering his tracks," Laurie contradicted.

I summed the situation up. "Both men heard about what Mrs Clack had found. Both men disappeared in a hurry. One of them realised that he would have to shut her up in case she *had* seen him in the woods, and in case she wittered on about it and someone actually believed her. For his own safety, the woman had to be silenced."

Frobisher chewed his lip, thinking hard about what Laurie had outlined. It was almost as if I could hear the rusty cogwheels in his limited brain creaking and grinding into gear.

"Sounds plausible," he said with a grudging sigh. "But which one of them did the killing? There are as yet unidentified fingerprints on one of the cups on her table. And we're still waiting for a result from that whisky bottle that was in the woods, though that could be circumstantial evidence. I suspect it'll have O'Connor's dabs all over it. We'll know if they belong to de Lainé once we get him to Barnstaple."

He stopped talking, swore under his breath, stood. "You should have told me all this ages ago. We've only arrested de Lainé. We need to bring the racehorse trainer in as well." He cursed again, louder this time, realising there had been an almighty error made. "I need to use your phone."

"Go ahead," Laurie said, getting to his feet and escorting the detective sergeant indoors, before returning to join me beneath the gazebo.

"I'd have thought it obvious to arrest *both* men," Laurie said in a lowered voice. "But what do I know, eh?"

DS Frobisher came back, looking as white as the proverbial linen sheet. He sat down heavily, asked in a shaking voice if he could possibly have more coffee, please. (Yes, he actually said *please*!) Something was clearly wrong.

"What is it?" Laurie enquired. "What's happened?"

Frobisher gulped a mouthful of coffee, wiped the residue from his lips. "It seems that we have a complication. The constables sent to fetch de Lainé in found something they'd not expected."

Laurie rolled his eyes. "Done a bunk has he?"

Frobisher shook his head. "No. Jack Woollen's hanged himself in one of the empty stables."

24

AFTERMATH

The frustrating thing was that we did not hear any more until several days later. We had no reason to; Devon's police were nothing to do with Laurie, Uncle Toby was back home in Chingford, and we couldn't very well waltz into Barnstaple police station and demand to know what was happening, could we? And even then, it was weeks later that the coroner's inquest took place, with the accompanying release of events finally made public.

It was all rather sad and horrid.

Oliver de Lainé, under arrest, had broken down and confessed everything. His acting career was well and truly over and he was up to his eyebrows in debt. He'd not worked, beyond small, insignificant bit-parts, for several years. He bluffed his way in front of others, keeping up his public star status, but desperately needed money. He'd appealed to his secret cousin, but Jack Woollen, too, was rapidly declining into financial difficulties.

Along came a less than straight Irish jockey, and between them they came up with a plan to make themselves a mint. A plan which went well until

O'Connor demanded a higher share of the profits, which between de Lainé and Jack Woollen were eroding away on a grand scale as they tried to keep their public heads above water, and the mounting debts at bay.

Despite achieving money from fixing races, by a mixture of frauds, like ensuring a favourite would consistently win, then suddenly he loses, bringing a higher pay-back from betting on everything else in the race, or making it seem that a horse was unlikely to win because he was agitated and sweating up (soap rubbed into the coat – result, white froth), then the horse romps home at good betting odds. Or fixing a race by deliberately slowing down, or falling off. Whatever methods they used the money went out faster than they raked it in. O'Connor became more and more greedy and demanding for his share, until one morning, in the quiet seclusion of the woods he'd been expecting to be generously paid what he reckoned he was owed. Received instead, a different reward. One that was nowhere near as expected or welcome.

De Lainé was supposed to have met him there in secret. O'Connor had waited, with a bottle of whisky supplied by his boss. De Lainé had never turned up; Jack Woollen had.

Fingerprints gave evidence of who had calmly been drinking tea with poor Dorothy Clack before strangling her, an innocent who had put both feet well and truly in the mire by going on and on about her nonsense fantasies and being so interested in watching the badgers. Jack Woollen could not be certain that she'd not seen him in the woods. There was only one way to make sure that she kept quiet.

An expert had thoroughly deciphered the contents of the black book, and it was reckoned that between them, the three men had cheated the racing world of a lot of money. Not that their winnings had done them any good, as the debts to the training yard alone had taken most of the haul, with de Lainé's amount owed to various people, taking what was left.

Stricken with remorse, unable to pay what he owed to owners, staff, creditors, vets, farriers, forage merchants, seemingly everyone in the county, Jack Woollen had hanged himself. They had found his confession, written in scrawled, drunken, handwriting in his jacket pocket.

He had come to the conclusion that a quick death was better than the disgrace and a life sentence in jail for two murders.

I couldn't help feeling sorry for him. He had seemed such a nice man, but then, many criminals, on the outside, seem to be nice men until their inner greed or nastiness gets the better of them.

Thank goodness for good policemen who take their job seriously and who protect us from the bad guys.

POSTSCRIPT

When I found all my old diaries in the attic during the tiresome days of Covid lockdown in 2020, I had initially wondered about destroying them. But then I realised, with changing a few names and places they could make interesting reading for interested readers, so here I am, transcribing my long-ago memories into these mystery tales.

Ralph Greenslade's youngest son and grandchildren run Lower Valley View Farm now. There are still horses at Four Horseshoes, but it is a prosperous riding school and trekking centre, not a racehorse training yard. Oliver de Lainé served his time for fraud, but in jail found a new vocation as a writer. His script for a film about a betting scam at the races won him an Oscar for best screenplay.

Dorothy Clack's cottage went up for sale when her husband was eventually found living a different life with a different woman. I know who bought the cottage, but the telling of that is not for *this* tale. Heather still lives in Chappletawton, but retired quite a while ago and no longer runs the shop. She is the mainstay of various village committees, though, and is very much an important and valued member of the village community.

But I'll tell you more about the village, its inhabitants and various goings-on in another story, another time. Until then, take care,

AUTHOR'S NOTE AND
ACKNOWLEDGEMENTS

This is a work of fiction, but for those interested in detail: South Chingford Branch Library, where Jan worked, was a real public library. The building (at the time of writing this – 2023) is still there in Hall Lane, but it is no longer a library. I worked there from 1969 when I left Wellington Avenue Secondary School for Girls at the age of sixteen, until 1982. I have many memories of the library – some good, some not so good, such is life when working for the public.

My family moved to Devon from northeast London in January 2013, buying an eighteenth-century stone-built, beamed ceilinged, farmhouse and accompanying land. Valley View Farm is very loosely based on my home. Top Meadow, where Jan helped with the hay is real, as is the haymaking – the front cover of this Cosy Mystery is that meadow, our 'Top Field'. My thanks to Andrew, our farmer neighbour for advising me on some of the detail.

As much as I have been able, I have checked and researched the various details mentioned about the early 1970s to ensure they are at least reasonably accurate, however, I cannot guarantee that everything is right, and some things I have deliberately left as contemporary with 2023 for personal nostalgia. The Tarka Line of the Great Western Railway System is an example, as it was not known by this name until relatively recently, but I have used it because I'm fond of this line – 'Tarka' being immortalised in 1927 by Henry Williamson's beautifully descriptive novel *Tarka the Otter*.

Like Jan mentions, I can see a small section of the

railway line from my bedroom window – watching a train go along the valley *is* somewhat like having your own life-size model railway. Add to that, before I moved to Devon, I used to visit my, then, editor Jo, who lived not far from Barnstaple, so I passed by my house on those journeys, unaware that I would move into it one day.

The Devon village is sort of my village, but not quite. Chappletawton (a fictional name) is larger than my village of Chittlehamholt, and we have a community shop run by volunteers – which replaced the original village shop and post office when it closed down prior to 2012. All the village characters in this murder mystery are entirely fictional, apart from my friend Heather, who has given her full permission to be included. The Exeter Inn is a real, award-winning, wonderful old pub, complete with a fox stalking two pheasants atop the thatch, while within, it is a homely, welcoming place to relax and enjoy yourself – and is frequented by several benign ghosts. As a thank you for Hazel and Steve's welcoming friendship, and the pleasure they bring to the village I wanted to include them as resident characters in my mysteries, so, as with Heather, with their permission I have transported them back in time to become the pub's custodians during the 1970s. I do heartily recommend the Exeter Inn's hospitality!

https://chittlehamholtvillage.blogspot.com/

Valley View Lane, the farms and the Four Horseshoes training yard are fictional, as is the footpath leading from the village through the woods down to the valley, and to the best of my knowledge, there are no leprechauns anywhere (although there is the ghost of a Sabre-Toothed Tiger). No 'plane went down near the village during World War II, and there is no headstone in a clearing – which also does not exist.

Newton Abbot Racecourse dates back to the 1800s, but the grandstand was built in 1969. I've had a delightful time looking at their You Tube races for inspiration but the horses' names I've used are, to the best of my knowledge, fictional. Ditto Jack Woollen and Ruairi O'Connor.

Money. A £5 note went a long way back in 1972, today the equivalent would be a little over £70. My first pay packet in 1969 was just over £100. I thought I was rich.

I mention ticks in the long grass and cut hay. They are particularly prevalent here in Devon, so please, if out walking do wear trousers or long socks. Lyme Disease was discovered in 1975, is caused by tick bites, is very unpleasant and can cause serious medical problems if undetected and untreated. Myxomatosis was, and sadly still is, an extremely horrible disease *intentionally* introduced into the rabbit population in the 1950s, and alas, has now also spread to hares. We do occasionally find a poor rabbit suffering dreadfully in our fields. We dispatch them as soon as we can, the kindest thing we can do for them, otherwise it is a slow, lingering death.

I have included a few very old TV programmes, which (with my apologies) US readers will probably not be familiar with: *The Woodentops, Andy Pandy* and such. These were children's favourites when I was young. I watched them in black and white on a small screen, box-like TV set. I think I was about five when I sat on the backdoor step one summer afternoon, trying to learn to whistle just like the boy in *The Woodentops*. *Dad's Army* is also mentioned, the repeats are still frequently aired, and they remain hilariously funny. Also for USA or foreign readers who are not familiar with British colloquial references, I have used some phrases that were common in the pre-1980s – 'burst my boiler' (desperate for a wee) for instance, and 'spend a penny' which is only really used by us 'oldies' now. It refers to the days of public toilets when you had to put 1d (1 penny pre-decimal) in the slot to gain entry into a cubicle ... hence 'spend a penny'.

'Button B' in a public red telephone box – there were two buttons to press when making a telephone call: you would put the required coins into the coin slot, dial the number you wanted and press Button A if the call was answered in order for the money to be 'collected', and for you to be heard. (The person on the other end would hear a beeping sound.) Or if there was no answer you'd press Button B to get your money back.

For French speakers, before you shout at me: 'Woollen' in French is 'de laine' with no accent (u*n pull de laine* is a woollen jumper). However, Oliver wanted to have an exotic-looking name, so he added the accent. And for my French readers, it makes a cheeky red herring! A quick thank you to Cathy Helms for her patience and expertise in designing the covers of my books and for formatting the text. Thank you to my Beta Readers, Cathy, Liz, Marian, Alison and Nicky, who picked up several bloopers. (I hope there are none remaining.) And especially to Annie for her copy-edit and final proof editing.

My thanks to the Wright Property, estate agents (Barnstaple and South Molton, formerly known as Geoffrey Clapp Estate Agency) for permission to use their photograph for the cover. The original was used by the estate agent for the sales brochure for our house. It's such a lovely photo – and a lovely field that yields generous crops of hay, and at present, also houses a number of beehives.

Finally, I began writing this Jan Christopher Mystery series during the 2020/21 lockdowns of the

Covid-19 pandemic as I wanted to write something different from my usual novels. I wanted something entertaining and fun for me to write and for you to read. I hope I have succeeded.

As an addendum: just like Jan, I did climb up our waterfall in our woods back in 2013 when I was more sprightly than I am these years later. Like her, I got a bit wet...

Helen Hollick
Devon 2023

HAYMAKING IN TOP MEADOW

Haymaking in Top Meadow
© Helen Hollick

COMING NEXT
The Jan Christopher Murder Mysteries
Episode #5 *A MEMORY OF MURDER*

ABOUT THE AUTHOR

Helen Hollick and her husband and daughter moved from north-east London in January 2013 after finding an eighteenth-century North Devon farmhouse through being a 'victim' on BBC TV's popular *Escape to The Country* show. The thirteen-acre property was the first one she was shown – and it was love at first sight. She enjoys her new rural life, and has a variety of animals on the farm, including Exmoor ponies and her daughter's string of show jumpers.

First accepted for publication by William Heinemann in 1993 – a week after her fortieth birthday – Helen then became a USA Today Bestseller with her historical novel, *The Forever Queen* (titled *A Hollow Crown in the UK*) with the sequel, *Harold the King* (US: *I Am the Chosen King*), novels that explore the events that led to the Battle of Hastings in 1066. Her *Pendragon's Banner Trilogy* is a fifth-century version of the Arthurian legend, and she also writes a pirate-based nautical adventure/fantasy series, *The Sea Witch Voyages*. Despite being impaired by the visual disorder of Glaucoma, she is also branching out into the quick read novella, 'Cosy Mystery' genre with the *Jan Christopher Mysteries*, set in the 1970s, with the first in the series, *A Mirror Murder* incorporating her, often hilarious, memories of working for thirteen years as a library assistant. Her non-fiction books are *Pirates: Truth and Tales* and *Life of a Smuggler*.

She runs a news and events blog for her village, assists where she can with her daughter's showjumpers– and occasionally gets time to write...

Website: www.helenhollick.net
Amazon Author Page (Universal Link):
http://viewauthor.at/HelenHollick
Newsletter Subscription:
http://tinyletter.com/HelenHollick
Blog: www.ofhistoryandkings.blogspot.com
Mastodon: https://mastodonapp.uk/@HelenHollick
Facebook: www.facebook.com/HelenHollickAuthor
Twitter: @HelenHollick

ALSO BY HELEN HOLLICK

THE PENDRAGON'S BANNER TRILOGY

The Kingmaking: Book One

Pendragon's Banner: Book Two

Shadow of the King: Book Three

THE SAXON 1066 SERIES

A Hollow Crown (UK edition title)

The Forever Queen (US edition title. USA Today bestseller)

Harold the King (UK edition title)

I Am The Chosen King (US edition title)

1066 Turned Upside Down

(alternative short stories by various authors)

THE SEA WITCH VOYAGES OF
CAPTAIN JESAMIAH ACORNE

Sea Witch: The first voyage

Pirate Code: The second voyage

Bring It Close: The third voyage

Ripples In The Sand: The fourth voyage

On The Account: The fifth voyage

Gallows Wake: The sixth voyage

When The Mermaid Sings

A short read prequel to the Sea Witch Voyages

Coffee Pot Book Club Book of the Year 2022

BRONZE AWARD WINNER

To follow

Jamaica Gold: The seventh voyage

BETRAYAL

Short stories by various authors

(including a Jesamiah Acorne adventure)

NON-FICTION

Pirates: Truth and Tales

Life Of A Smuggler: In Fact And Fiction

BEFORE YOU GO

How To Say 'Thank you' to your favourite authors
(Feedback is so important, and we do appreciate your
comments.)

Leave a review on Amazon
http://viewauthor.at/HelenHollick

'Like' and 'follow' where you can

Subscribe to a newsletter

Buy a copy of your favourite book as a present

Spread the word!

Printed in Great Britain
by Amazon

25865582R00091